PENGUIN CLASSICS
Maigret's Dead Man

'I love reading Simenon. He makes me think of Chekhov'
– William Faulkner

'A truly wonderful writer . . . marvellously readable – lucid,
simple, absolutely in tune with the world he creates'
– Muriel Spark

'Few writers have ever conveyed with such a sure touch, the
bleakness of human life'   – A. N. Wilson

'One of the greatest writers of the twentieth century . . .
Simenon was unequalled at making us look inside, though
the ability was masked by his brilliance at absorbing us obses-
sively in his stories'   – *Guardian*

'A novelist who entered his fictional world as if he were part
of it'   – Peter Ackroyd

'The greatest of all, the most genuine novelist we have had
in literature'   – André Gide

'Superb . . . The most addictive of writers . . . A unique teller
of tales'   – *Observer*

'The mysteries of the human personality are revealed in all
their disconcerting complexity'   – Anita Brookner

'A writer who, more than any other crime novelist, combined
a high literary reputation with popular appeal' – P. D. James

'A supreme writer . . . Unforgettable vividness' – *Independent*

'Compelling, remorseless, brilliant'   – John Gray

'Extraordinary masterpieces of the twentieth century'
– John Banville

GEORGES SIMENON

Maigret's Dead Man

Translated by DAVID COWARD

PENGUIN BOOKS

PENGUIN CLASSICS

UK | USA | Canada | Ireland | Australia
India | New Zealand | South Africa

Penguin Books is part of the Penguin Random House group of companies
whose addresses can be found at global.penguinrandomhouse.com.

Penguin
Random House
UK

First published in French as *Maigret et son mort* by Presses de la Cité 1948
This translation first published 2016

011

Set in Dante MT Std 12.5/15pt
Typeset by Palimpsest Book Production Limited, Falkirk, Stirlingshire

Printed in Great Britain by Clays Ltd, Elcograf s.p.A

ISBN: 978-0-241-20637-9

www.greenpenguin.co.uk

MIX
Paper from
responsible sources
FSC® C018179

Penguin Random House is committed to a
sustainable future for our business, our readers
and our planet. This book is made from Forest
Stewardship Council® certified paper.

Maigret's Dead Man

1.

'Let me stop you there, madame . . .'

After minutes of patient effort, Maigret finally managed to interrupt his visitor's flow.

'You are now telling me that your daughter is slowly poisoning you . . .'

'It's true . . .'

'But a moment ago, you said, no less categorically, that it was your son-in-law who deliberately lay in wait in the corridor for the chambermaid to pass so that he could slip poison into either your coffee or one of your many varieties of herbal tea . . .'

'Quite true . . .'

'Even so . . .' – he consulted, or pretended to consult, the notes he had taken of this interview, which had been going on for more than an hour – 'when you began, you told me that your daughter and her husband hate each other . . .'

'That is also true, inspector.'

'But they are agreed that they want to do away with you?'

'No, not at all! Don't you see, they are both trying to poison me *separately*?'

'What about your niece, Rita?'

'Also separately . . .'

It was February. The weather was mild and sunny with

the occasional cloud plump with showers which brought sudden rains down out of the sky. But three times since his visitor had been in his office, Maigret had poked his stove, the last remaining stove in the Police Judiciaire building, which he had had to fight so hard to keep when central heating had been installed throughout Quai des Orfèvres.

The woman was probably roasting in her mink coat, under the silk of her black dress, under the accumulation of jewels which decorated her all over – ears, throat, wrists and bosom – making her look like a gypsy. And it was also of a gypsy that she made you think, not of a grand lady, with her violent make-up which had formed into a crust and was now beginning to run.

'So that makes three people in all who are intending to poison you.'

'Not intending . . . They've already started . . .'

'And you claim that they're all acting independently of each other . . .'

'I'm not claiming anything, I am sure of it.'

She spoke with the same Romanian accent as a famous Boulevard actress and with the same sudden passionate outbursts which set her quivering.

'I am not mad . . . Read this . . . I assume you've heard of Professor Touchard? . . . He's the one they always call as an expert witness in all the important trials . . .'

She had thought of everything. She had even consulted the most famous psychiatrist in Paris and requested him to supply a document certifying that she was in her right mind!

There was nothing he could do but listen to her patiently and, to keep her happy, jot down a few notes from time to time on his pad. She had arranged her visit through a government minister who had personally phoned the commissioner of the Police Judiciaire. Her husband, who had died a few weeks earlier, had been a councillor of state. She lived in Rue de Presbourg in one of those enormous stone-built mansions which front Place de l'Étoile.

'As for my son-in-law, this is how he carries on . . . I've looked carefully into it . . . I've been watching him for months . . .'

'So he began when your husband was still alive?'

She handed him a plan, which she had drawn with great care, of the first floor of the house.

'My bedroom is marked A . . . B is the bedroom of my daughter and her husband . . . But for some time Gaston has not been sleeping in that room . . .'

The phone – at last! – which offered Maigret a moment's respite.

'Hello? . . . Who is on the line? . . .'

Normally the officer on the police switchboard did not put through any but the most urgent calls.

'I'm sorry, sir . . . It's a man. He won't give his name but is very insistent. Says he must absolutely talk to you . . . He swears it's a matter of life and death . . .'

'And he wants to speak to me personally?'

'Yes . . . Shall I put him through?'

Maigret heard a voice saying anxiously:

'Hello? . . . Is that you? . . .'

'Detective Chief Inspector Maigret, yes . . .'

'I'm sorry about this . . . My name wouldn't mean any-thing to you . . . You don't know me, but you used to know my wife, Nine . . . Hello? . . . I've got to tell you it all very quickly because any time now something might happen that . . .'

Maigret's first reaction was to think: 'Oh God, not another lunatic! It must be the day for them . . .'

He had observed that lunatics came in waves, as if they were affected by the phases of the moon. He made a mental note that later he would consult a calendar.

'My first thought was to come and see you . . . I walked past Quai des Orfèvres but didn't dare go in because he was right behind me . . . I think he would have had no hesitation in shooting me . . .'

'Who are you talking about?'

'Hang on. I'm quite close. Just across from your office. A minute ago I could see your window. Quai des Grands-Augustins. There's a small bar, you'll know it, it's called Aux Caves du Beaujolais. I'm calling from the phone booth there . . . Hello? . . . Can you hear me? . . .'

It was 11.30 in the morning, and Maigret automatically jotted the time down in his notepad, then the name of the bar . . .

'I've thought of every conceivable solution . . . I approached a policeman on Place du Châtelet . . .'

'When?'

'Half an hour ago. One of the men was very close. It was the small, dark one. There are several of them, they work in relays. I'm not sure if I could recognize them all. But I know the small dark man is one of them . . .'

Then silence.

'Hello?' said Maigret.

The silence continued for several moments, then the voice came again:

'Sorry. I heard someone coming into the bar and thought it was him. I opened the door an inch but it was only a delivery man . . . Hello? . . .'

'What did you say to the policeman?'

'That some men had been following me since last night . . . No, actually since yesterday afternoon . . . And that they must be waiting for an opportunity to kill me . . . I asked him to arrest the one who was standing behind me . . .'

'And he refused?'

'He asked me to point the man out, and when I turned round to do so I couldn't see him. So he didn't believe me. I made the most of the opportunity and ran down into the Métro. I jumped on the first train and then jumped off it again just before the doors closed, as it was about to leave. I walked along all the passages. I came out opposite the department store, Bazar de l'Hôtel-de-Ville and walked through all the shops too . . .'

He must have been walking very briskly, even running, because his breathing was still rapid and wheezy.

'What I'm asking is for you to send a plainclothes officer to me right away. Here, in the Caves du Beaujolais. He mustn't speak to me. He must act all casual. I'll leave. I'm pretty sure the man tailing me will follow. He can then be arrested, and I'll come to see you and explain everything . . .'

'Hello?'

'I said I . . .'

Then nothing. Confused sounds.

'Hello? . . . Hello? . . .'

But there was no one at the other end of the line.

When she saw Maigret hang up, the old woman who was being poisoned resumed imperturbably: 'As I was saying . . .'

'Excuse me for a moment, would you?'

He went to the door which communicated with the office occupied by the inspectors.

'Janvier, put your hat on and run over to Quai des Grands-Augustins. There's a small bar there, Aux Caves du Beaujolais it's called. Ask if the man who just used the phone is still there.'

He lifted the receiver of his phone.

'Get me the Caves du Beaujolais . . .'

As he did so, he looked out of the window. On the opposite bank of the Seine, where Quai des Grands-Augustins rises to the level of Pont Saint-Michel, he had a clear view of the narrow front of a bar which catered mostly for regulars. He had occasionally stopped there to drink a beer at the counter. He remembered that there was a step down to go in, that it was cool inside and that the landlord always wore a cellar man's black apron.

A lorry parked outside the bar blocked his view of the door. Pedestrians passed by on the pavement.

'You see, inspector . . .'

'One moment, madame, please . . .'

Still looking out, he very carefully filled his pipe.

This old woman, with her tales of poison, would waste his entire morning for him, if not more. She had brought with her reams of paper, plans, certificates, even analyses of various kinds of foodstuffs which she must have ordered from her own pharmacist.

'I've always been a mistrustful sort of person, you know . . .'

She gave off a powerful, nauseating perfume which had invaded the office and had managed to get the better of the wholesome smell of pipe smoke.

'Hello? . . . Haven't you got that number I asked you for yet?'

'I'm calling it, sir. I haven't stopped calling it. The number is constantly engaged. Unless someone forgot to put the receiver back on the hook . . .'

Moments later, Janvier, not wearing a jacket, crossed the bridge in an ungainly lope and went into the bar. The lorry decided to drive off, but Maigret still could not see inside the bar as it was too dark. A few more moments elapsed, then the phone rang . . .

'There, sir. I've got that number for you. It's ringing now.'

'Hello? . . . Who is this? Is that you, Janvier? . . . The phone was off the hook? . . . Well?'

'Yes, there was a shortish man here phoning . . .'

'Did you see him?'

'No. He'd gone by the time I got here. Apparently he

kept looking out through the window of the booth and opening the door . . .'

'Anything else?'

'A customer walked in, and the first thing he did was look towards the phone booth. Then he ordered a brandy at the counter. As soon as the man in the booth saw him, he broke off his conversation.'

'Did both of them leave?'

'Yes, one behind the other.'

'Try to get the landlord to give you as detailed a description as possible of both men . . . Hello? And while you're at it come back via Place du Châtelet. Question all the officers on duty. Try and find out if one of them, about three-quarters of an hour ago, was approached by the same shortish man who asked him to arrest someone who was following him.'

When he hung up, the old woman looked at him with satisfaction and evident approval, as though she were about to award him a very good mark:

'Now that's exactly how I understand policemen operate. You don't waste any time. You think of everything.'

He sat down again with a sigh. He had been about to open the window because he was beginning to suffocate in his overheated office, but he did not want to miss any opportunity of cutting short the visit of this woman who had been recommended by the minister.

Aubain-Vasconcelos. That was her name. It would remain engraved on his memory, even if he never saw her again. Did she die in the days immediately following? Probably not. He would have heard about it. Perhaps she had been locked away? Perhaps she had felt let down by the official police and had instead turned to a private detective agency? Or perhaps she had woken up next morning with some other fixation?

Be that as it may, he was stuck there for another hour listening to her talking about all the people in that vast mansion in Rue de Presbourg – where life could not have been much fun – who were feeding her poison at all hours of the day.

At noon he was at long last able to open his window. Then, pipe between his teeth, he walked into the commissioner's office.

'Did you get rid of her gently?'

'As gently as could be.'

'I gather that in her day she was one of the most beautiful women in Europe. I knew her husband slightly, the mildest, dullest, most boring man imaginable. Are you going out, Maigret?'

He hesitated. The streets were beginning to smell of spring. Tables and chairs had been brought out on to the terrace of the Brasserie Dauphine and the commissioner's question was an invitation to stroll down for a pre-prandial drink.

'I think I'd better stay here. I got a very odd phone call this morning.'

He was about to explain when the phone rang. The commissioner answered then passed him the receiver.

'It's for you.'

Maigret recognized the voice immediately. It sounded even more frightened than before.

'Hello! We were interrupted earlier. He came in. He could have heard through the door of the phone booth. I was scared . . .'

'Where are you now?'

'In the Tabac des Vosges, on the corner of Place des Vosges and Rue des Francs-Bourgeois. I tried to give him the slip. I don't know if I managed to. But I swear I'm not mistaken, that he really is out to kill me. It would take too long to explain. I thought the others wouldn't take me seriously, but that you . . .'

'Hello?'

'He's here . . . I . . . Sorry . . .'

The commissioner stared at Maigret, who was wearing his irritated look.

'Something wrong?'

'I don't know. This is a very strange business. Do you mind if . . . ?'

He picked up another phone.

'Get me the Tabac des Vosges at once . . . The owner, yes . . .'

Then, to the commissioner:

'Provided this time he didn't forget to hang up.'

The phone rang almost straight away.

'Hello . . . Is that the Tabac des Vosges? Am I speaking to the owner? . . . Is the customer who just phoned still there? . . . What was that? . . . Yes, you go and check . . . Hello? . . . Just left? . . . Did he pay? . . . Tell me – did another customer come in while he was on the phone? . . . No? . . . On the terrace? . . . Go and look if he's still there . . . He left too? . . . And without waiting for the

drink he'd ordered? . . . Thanks . . . No . . . Who am I? . . .
Police . . . No, nothing for you to worry about . . .'

It was at this point that he decided not to go to the Brasserie Dauphine with the commissioner. When he opened the door of the inspectors' office, he found Janvier, who was back and waiting for him.

'Come into my office. Tell me everything.'

'He's an oddball, sir. Shortish and nondescript, wore a raincoat, a grey hat and black shoes. He rushed into the Caves du Beaujolais and made straight for the phone booth, telling the man behind the counter to serve him a drink. He said, "Anything'll do". Through the window of the booth, the bar owner saw him talking animatedly and waving his arms about. Then, when the other customer walked in, the first one shot out of the booth like an imp out of a bottle, without saying a word and headed off quickly towards Place Saint-Michel . . .'

'What about the second man?'

'He was short too . . . Anyway not very big, but strong, jet black hair.'

'What about the uniformed officer in Place du Châtelet?'

'It did happen. The man in the raincoat approached him, out of breath, looking wild-eyed. He waved his arms about and asked him to arrest someone who was following him but he couldn't point him out in the crowd. The officer decided to make a note of it in his report, just in case.'

'I want you to go to Place des Vosges. There's a tobacconist's on the corner of Rue des Francs-Bourgeois.'

'Got it . . .'

A shortish man, waves his arms about, wears a beige raincoat and a grey hat. That was the sum total of all that was known about him. There was nothing else to do now but stand by the window and watch the crowds stream out of offices and invade the bars, the pavement cafés and the restaurants. Paris was all light and life. As always happens, more pleasure was taken around the middle of February in the first gusts of spring than when spring finally arrived. And the newspapers would doubtless soon be talking of the famous chestnut tree on Boulevard Saint-Germain, which would be in flower a month from now.

Maigret phoned down to the Brasserie Dauphine.

'Hello? . . . Joseph? . . . Maigret . . . Can you bring me up a couple of beers and some sandwiches? . . . That's right, for one . . .'

Before the sandwiches arrived, the phone rang. He recognized the voice at once: he had told the switchboard to put these calls through immediately, without wasting a moment.

'Hello? This time I think I've well and truly given him the slip . . .'

'Who are you?'

'Nine's husband. But that's not important. There are at least four of them, not counting the woman . . . Someone absolutely must come at once and . . .'

This time, he hadn't had time to say where he was phoning from. Maigret called the woman at the exchange. It took a few minutes. The call had come from the Quatre Sergents de la Rochelle, a restaurant on Boulevard Beaumarchais, at no distance from the Bastille.

This location wasn't very far from Place des Vosges either. It was possible to track the meanderings of the shortish man in a raincoat within, or almost, the same neighbourhood of Paris.

'Hello? Is that you Janvier? . . . I thought you might still be there . . .'

Maigret was phoning him at the bar in Place des Vosges.

'Go to the Quatre Sergents de la Rochelle . . . Yes . . . Keep the taxi . . .'

An hour went by without a single phone call, without anything more being learned about Nine's husband. When the phone did ring, it wasn't him at the other end of the line but a café waiter.

'Hello? Am I speaking to Detective Chief Inspector Maigret? . . . Inspector Maigret in person? . . . I am the waiter at the Café de Birague in Rue de Birague. I'm speaking on behalf of a customer who asked me to call you.'

'How long ago was this?'

'Maybe a quarter of an hour. I was supposed to phone straight away but it's our busy time.'

'A shortish man, wearing a raincoat?'

'Yes. Right. I was afraid it was some sort of practical joke. He was in a terrible hurry. He kept looking out into the street . . . Wait, I want to get this right . . . As I remember, in his own words, he said to tell you that he'd try to lead the man to the Canon de la Bastille. Do you know it? It's the brasserie on the corner of Boulevard Henri IV. He wanted you to send somebody pronto . . . Wait, that's not all. I expect you'll understand. He said, and these are his exact words: "It's a different man. Now it's the tall one with red hair, he's the worst."'

Maigret went there himself. He got into a taxi, which took less than ten minutes to reach Place de la Bastille. The brasserie was a great barn of a place and quiet. Its customers were mostly regulars who ordered the dish of the day or a plate of charcuterie. He looked round for a man in a raincoat, then toured the coat racks hoping to spot a beige raincoat.

'Tell me, waiter . . .'

There were six waiters plus the woman at the till and the man who owned the place. He questioned them all. No one had seen his man. So he took a seat in a corner by the door, ordered a beer and waited, smoking his pipe. Half an hour later, sandwiches notwithstanding, he ordered a plate of sauerkraut and frankfurters. He watched people pass by on the pavement. Every time a raincoat appeared, he gave a start, and there were many of them, for the shower now falling was the third since that morning. The rain was translucent, transparent, the plain, innocent kind of rain which does not prevent the sun from shining.

'Hello? . . . Police Judiciaire? . . . It's Maigret. Has Janvier got back? Let me speak to him . . . Is that you, Janvier? . . . Jump in a taxi and meet me in the Canon de la Bastille . . . You're right, today's the day for bars. I'll wait for you here . . . No, nothing new . . .'

Too bad if the man with the windmill arms was a hoaxer. Maigret left his inspector to keep an eye on the

Canon de la Bastille and used the taxi to go back to his office.

The chances that Nine's husband had been murdered since half past twelve were slim, because he did not seem keen to venture down backstreets. On the contrary, he chose busy parts of town and main thoroughfares. Even so, Maigret contacted the emergency services, which kept constantly up to date about any trouble that happened in Paris.

'If you are informed that a man in a raincoat has had an accident or been involved in an argument or whatever, give me a ring . . .'

He also gave instructions for one of the Police Judiciaire's squad cars to be kept available for him in the courtyard of Quai des Orfèvres. This was perhaps excessive, but he was merely stacking the odds on his side.

He talked to people who came to his office, smoked many pipes and stoked his stove from time to time, while keeping his window open, and occasionally aimed a reproachful look at his phone, which remained resolutely silent.

'You used to know my wife . . .' the man had said.

He tried idly to remember a Nine. He must have met many of that name. He had known one, a few years before, who ran a small bar in Cannes, but she had been an old lady even then and was probably dead by now. There was also a niece of his wife's whose name was Aline, but everybody called her Nine.

'Hello? Detective Chief Inspector Maigret?'

It was four o'clock. It was still broad daylight but the

inspector had switched on his desk lamp with the green shade.

'I am the postmaster at 28, Rue du Faubourg Saint-Denis. I'm sorry to bother you. It's probably some sort of hoax. A few minutes ago a customer approached the counter that deals with registered parcels . . . Hello? . . . The counter-clerk, Mademoiselle Denfer, told me that he seemed to be in a great hurry. He kept turning round. He pushed a piece of paper under her nose. He said: "Don't try to understand. Phone this message through to Inspector Maigret at once." Then he vanished into the crowd.

'The member of staff concerned reported this to me. I have the piece of paper in front of me. It's written in pencil, a terrible scrawl. Looks like the man wrote the note while he was walking along.

'This is what it says: "I couldn't make it to the Canon". Does that mean anything to you? It's meaningless to me. But no matter. Then there's a word I can't read. "Now there's two of them. The small dark one has come back." It's the word "dark" I'm not sure of . . . Say again? . . . Fair enough, if that's what you think it says . . . There's more: "I'm sure they've decided to get me today. I'm not far from the Quai. But they're cunning. Warn your officers to be on their guard."

'That's it. If you want, I'll send the note by telegram messenger . . . By taxi? Most certainly. Provided that you bear the cost, because I cannot undertake . . .'

'Hello? . . . Janvier? . . . You can come back now.'

Half an hour later the two of them sat smoking in

Maigret's office, where a small round patch of red showed under the stove.

'I expect you managed to find time to have lunch?'

'I had sauerkraut and frankfurters at the Canon . . .'

Him as well! Meantime, Maigret had alerted cycle-mounted patrols as well as the municipal police. Parisians who walked into department stores, jostled each other on pavements, flocked into cinemas or hurried down the steps of Métro stations, did not notice a thing. But hundreds of eyes scrutinized the crowds, pausing on anyone wearing a beige raincoat or sporting a grey hat.

There was another sharp shower at about five o'clock, when the number of pedestrians in and around the Châtelet reached its peak. The pavements glistened, a halo surrounded every streetlamp and along every kerb, at intervals of ten metres, people stood and raised their arms every time a taxi drove past.

'The landlord of the Caves du Beaujolais reckons he's thirty-five or forty. The man who runs the Tabac des Vosges puts him at about thirty. He's clean-shaven, rosy-cheeked and blue-eyed. As to what kind of man he is, I didn't manage to form any idea. I was told that *you see lots like him about* . . .'

Madame Maigret, who was having her sister to dinner, phoned at six to make sure her husband wouldn't be home late and to ask him to call in at the pâtisserie on his way home.

'Can you keep an eye on things here until nine? I'll get Lucas to replace you after that . . .'

Janvier was willing. There was nothing to do but wait.

'I want to be phoned at home if there are any developments.'

He did not forget to call in at the pâtisserie in Avenue de la République, the only one in Paris, said Madame Maigret, capable of making a decent mille-feuille. He kissed his sister-in-law, who as always smelled of lavender. They ate dinner. He drank a glass of calvados. Before walking Odette to the Métro, he rang the Police Judiciaire.

'Lucas? . . . Any news? . . . Are you still in my office?'

Lucas, ensconced in Maigret's own chair, probably had his feet propped up on the desk, reading.

'Just carry on as you are. Good night.'

As he walked back from the Métro station, Boulevard Richard-Lenoir was deserted, and his footsteps were loud on the pavement. Hearing other footsteps behind him, he stiffened, turned instinctively because he was thinking about his man who even now was perhaps still wandering through the streets, fearful, avoiding dark places, seeking safety in bars and cafés.

He fell asleep before his wife – so she said at least, as she always did, just as she also claimed that he snored – and the alarm-clock on the bedside table registered 2.20 when the phone dragged him from his sleep. It was Lucas.

'Maybe I'm disturbing you for nothing, sir. I haven't got many details yet. But the duty desk of the Police Emergency Service has just let me know that the body of a man has been found in Place de la Concorde. Near Quai des Tuileries. That's the jurisdiction of the first *arrondissement*. I've asked the main station there not to touch anything . . . What? . . . Fine. If you wish. I'll send a taxi for you.'

Madame Maigret sighed as she watched her husband who got into his trousers but couldn't find his shirt.

'Do you think you'll be gone long?'

'I don't know.'

'Couldn't you send one of your inspectors instead?'

When he opened the sideboard in the dining room, she knew he was about to pour himself a tot of calvados. Then he came back for his pipes, which he had forgotten.

The taxi was waiting for him. The Grands Boulevards were almost deserted. A huge moon, far brighter than usual, hung over the green dome of the Opera House.

Place de la Concorde. Two cars were parked one behind the other along the kerb, near the Tuileries Gardens, and shadowy figures came and went.

The first thing Maigret noticed as he got out of the taxi was the smudge made by a beige raincoat on the silvery pavement.

Then, as police officers in capes stepped aside and an inspector from the *arrondissement* advanced to meet him, he muttered:

'So it wasn't a hoax. They really did for him!'

The sound of lapping blew on a cool breeze off the Seine, which was no distance away. Traffic emerging from Rue Royale moved noiselessly towards the Champs-Élysées.

The electric sign outside Maxim's was a red presence in the night.

'Single wound with a knife, sir,' said Inspector Lequeux,

whom Maigret knew well. 'We were waiting for you before we moved him.'

What was it at that moment that gave Maigret the feeling that there was something here that was not quite right?

Place de la Concorde was too big, too light, too airy with, at its centre, the tall, bold white needle of the obelisk. None of this seemed to belong to the same world as the phone calls he had got that morning from the Caves du Beaujolais, the Tabac des Vosges and the Quatre Sergents on Boulevard Beaumarchais.

Up to and including that last call and the note handed in at the post office on Rue du Faubourg Saint-Denis, the man had confined himself to a part of town known for its narrow, well-populated streets.

Does a man who knows he is being followed, who senses there is a murderer breathing down his neck and is expecting the fatal blow to fall at any moment, suddenly switch to wide open spaces like Place de la Concorde?

'You'll find that he wasn't killed here . . .'

Confirmation would come an hour later when Officer Piedbœuf, who had been on duty outside a nightclub in Rue de Douai, filed his report.

A car had pulled up at the door of the club. In it were two men in dinner suits and two women in evening clothes. All four were in high spirits, slightly the worse for drink, one of the men in particular. As the others went inside, he turned on his heel and came back.

'Ah, officer . . . I don't know if I'm doing the right thing saying this, because I don't want to ruin our evening. But it can't be helped. You can make of it what you like. Just now, as we were driving across Place de la Concorde, the car in front of us stopped. I was driving and slowed, thinking that it had broken down. They pulled something out of the car and dumped it on the pavement. I think it was a body . . .

'The car was a yellow Citroën, with a Paris registration. The last two digits on the number plate were a 3 and an 8.'

2.

At what point did Nine's husband become Maigret's dead man, as he came to be known to everyone in the Police Judiciaire? Perhaps it happened with what might be called their first encounter that night in Place de la Concorde. Perhaps not, but Inspector Lequeux was very struck by the way Maigret had behaved. It was difficult to put a finger on why his reaction was not entirely normal. The police are used to dealing with violent death and unexpected corpses and handle them with professional detachment – or sometimes with black humour, in the manner of off-duty junior doctors. But then again, Maigret did not seem to be exactly grieving in the true sense of the word.

But why, for example, did he not begin by doing what seemed natural and bend over the corpse? Before doing so, he took several pulls on his pipe and stood in the middle of the group of uniformed police officers, chatting with Lequeux and glancing casually at a young woman wearing a lamé dress under a mink coat who had just got out of a car along with two men. She waited, her hand clutching the arm of one of the two men, as if something else was about to happen.

It was only after some time had gone by that he slowly headed towards the prone form of the beige smudge of the raincoat and leaned over it, still unhurriedly, as he would have done, as Inspector Lequeux would later say, if the body had been a relative or a friend.

And when he straightened up again, his eyebrows came together in a fierce scowl that made his anger abundantly clear. He asked questions with such venom that he seemed to be holding everyone present responsible.

'Who did this?'

Had it been done with fists or boots? There was no telling which. However it was obvious that before or after killing the man with a knife, someone had struck him repeatedly with such violence that his features were swollen, one lip had been split and the whole of one side of his face had been knocked out of shape.

'I'm waiting for the mortuary van,' said Lequeux.

Without the injuries, the man's face would have been unremarkable, fairly young and probably quite cheerful. Even in death, there were traces of something open and honest in his expression.

Why did the woman in mink seem so shaken by the sight of a foot wearing only a mauve sock? That shoeless foot looked incongruous lying on the pavement next to another foot encased in a shoe made of black kid leather. It was naked, private. It did not really seem dead. It was Maigret who retrieved the other shoe, which lay by the kerb six or seven metres away.

After that, he did not speak again. While he waited, he smoked. Curious bystanders mingled with the whispering group. Then the mortuary van pulled up at the kerb, and two attendants lifted the body. Underneath it the paving stones were bare, with no trace of blood.

'Just write up your report, Lequeux, and let me have it.'

Or was it now, as Maigret climbed into the front seat of the van and left the others to themselves, that he really took possession of the dead man?

That was how it was all night. That was how it still was the next morning. It was as if the body belonged to him, that this dead man was his dead man.

He had given instructions for Moers, one of the experts from Criminal Records, to wait for him in the Forensic Institute. Moers was young, thin and tall, with a face that never smiled and thick lenses which made his shy eyes look small.

'To work, Moers . . .'

He had also summoned Dr Paul, who was due to arrive at any moment. In addition to the two of them, there was only one attendant and, in their refrigerated cabinets, the anonymous dead of Paris collected during the past few days.

The light was raw, little was said and the movements of hands precise. They looked for all the world like conscientious workmen crouching over some delicate night-time task.

They found virtually nothing in the pockets. A packet of black tobacco and a tray of cigarette papers, a box of matches, a nondescript penknife, a key of a not-very-recent design, a pencil and a handkerchief with an initial on it. Some loose change in a trouser pocket but no wallet or any means of identification.

Moers removed the man's suit carefully piece by piece and put each one in a bag made of waxed paper, which he then closed securely. He then proceeded to do the same with the shirt, shoes and socks. All items were of average quality. The jacket bore the label of an outfitter's on Boulevard Sébastopol which sold ready-made clothes. The colour of the trousers, which were newer, was not a good match.

The dead man was naked when Dr Paul arrived, beard neatly trimmed and clear eyed, despite being called out in the middle of the night.

'Now, then, Maigret, what does this poor man have to say for himself?'

Because it was now all about making the dead man talk. It was routine. Normally, Maigret would have gone home to bed and would have found the various reports on his desk the next morning.

But this time he insisted on being there for everything, pipe in mouth, hands in pockets, bleary-eyed and half-asleep.

Before he could proceed, the doctor had to wait for the photographers, who were late. Moers made the most of the delay to clean the corpse's nails, hands and feet thoroughly, collect the smallest fragments and put them into small bags, on which he wrote cabbalistic signs.

'It won't be easy to make him look chirpy,' observed the photographer after inspecting the dead man's face.

It was all still routine work. First, photos of the body and the wound. Then, for publication in the newspapers for identification purposes, a photo of the face, which had to be made to look as lifelike as possible. That is why the mortician was busily applying make-up to the dead man, who, in the ice-cold light, looked even more deathly pale than ever, but with rosy cheeks and a mouth painted like a street-walker's.

'All yours, doc . . .'

'Are you staying, Maigret?'

He stayed to the end. It was 6.30 in the morning when Dr Paul and he went for a coffee in a little bar which had just opened its shutters.

'I take it you do not want to wait for my report . . . Tell me, is this an important case?'

'I don't know.'

All round them, workmen, their eyes still full of sleep, ate their croissants, and the early-morning fog pinned pearls of moisture on all their overcoats. It was chilly. In the street, pedestrians were preceded by thin clouds of steam. Lights went on in windows one after the other on the various floors of the houses.

'First, I can tell you that he was a man from an ordinary background . . .

'He probably had a poor childhood and was not particularly well looked after, if the evidence of bone and teeth formation is anything to go by. His hands do not indicate what kind of work he did. They are strong but relatively well cared for. He was probably not a manual labourer. Nor a clerk either, because his hands show no traces, however slight, of the deformities which reveal that a person has spent much time writing, either with a pen or a type-writer. On the other hand, his feet are sensitive, with low arches, which points to someone who spent most of his life standing up.'

Maigret did not take notes; the details were etched in his memory.

'We now turn to a crucial question: when the crime was committed. I can say without fear of contradiction that it took place between eight and ten last night.'

Maigret had already been informed by phone of the statements made by the late-night revellers and of the sighting of the yellow Citroën in Place de la Concorde shortly after one in the morning.

'Tell me, doctor, did you notice anything unusual?'

'What do you mean?'

The doctor with the almost legendary beard had been a pathologist for thirty-five years and he was more familiar with criminal investigations than most police officers.

'The crime was not committed in Place de la Concorde.'

'That's obvious.'

'It was probably committed in some out-of-the-way place.'

'Probably.'

'Usually, when people take the risk of moving a body, especially in a city like Paris, they are trying to hide it, to make it disappear or at least to delay the time when it is found.'

'You're right, Maigret. I hadn't thought of that.'

'But in this case, on the contrary, we have people prepared to risk being caught or at the very least giving us a lead, by dumping a corpse in the middle of Paris, in the most highly visible spot where, even in the middle of the night, it could not remain ten minutes without being found.'

'In other words, the murderers wanted it to be found. That's what you're thinking, am I right?'

'Not exactly. But it doesn't matter.'

'Even so, they took some steps to ensure the body could not easily be identified. The damage to the face was not done by bare fists but with a heavy instrument the nature of which I am not unfortunately able to determine.'

'Was it done before death?'

'After . . . A few minutes after.'

'Are you sure it was only minutes after?'

'Less than half an hour, I'd swear to it. But now, Maigret, there is another detail which I will probably not include in my report because I am not sure of my ground and have no wish to be challenged by lawyers when this business comes to court. I spent some time examining the wound, as you saw. Now, I've examined several hundred knife wounds in my time. I'd swear this one was not delivered unexpectedly.

'Imagine that there are two men standing, arguing about something. They are facing each other, and one of them stabs the other man. It would be impossible for him to make a wound like the one I've just examined. The blow was not to the victim's back, either.

'But suppose that a man is seated, or even standing, but with his mind fully occupied with something else. Someone could creep up quietly on him from behind, put one arm around him and with the other strike hard with the knife, choosing his spot exactly.

'Or to be even more specific, it's as if the victim had been tied up or held down so that he could not move, as if someone had then, literally, "carved" him . . . Are you with me?'

'I'm with you.'

But Maigret knew very well that Nine's husband had not been taken by surprise, for he had been eluding his murderers for twenty-four hours.

What for the doctor was a problem of a more or less theoretical nature was in Maigret's eyes a matter of much more immediate human import.

It so happened that he had heard the man's voice. He had almost seen him. He had certainly followed him step by step, bar by bar, on his mad progress through certain parts of Paris, always the same ones, in the area between Châtelet and Bastille.

The two men were now walking along the bank of the river, Maigret smoking his pipe and Dr Paul cigarette after cigarette – he smoked constantly while performing autopsies and would tell anyone who asked that tobacco is the best antiseptic. Dawn was just appearing in the sky. Strings of barges were beginning to pass down the Seine. Down-and-outs were seen, numbed by the night cold, climbing stiff-limbed up the steps from the embankment, where they had slept under a bridge.

'The man was killed shortly after his last meal, maybe immediately.'

'Do you know what he ate?'

'Pea soup, Provençal creamed salt cod-and-potato pie and an apple. He had drunk white wine. I also found traces of spirits in his stomach.'

Oddly enough, they were now passing in front of the

Caves du Beaujolais. The landlord had only just taken the wooden shutters inside. They could see the dark interior and caught the smell of stale wine.

'Are you going home now?' asked the doctor, who was about to hail a taxi.

'I'm going up to Criminal Records.'

The tall building on Quai des Orfèvres was almost empty. Teams of sweepers were at work in the corridors and on staircases, where the winter dampness still lingered.

In his office, Maigret found Lucas, who had just fallen asleep in his armchair.

'Any developments?'

'The papers have got the photo. Only a few will publish it in the morning edition because they didn't receive it early enough.'

'Anything on the car?'

'I'm looking into my third yellow Citroën, but none fit the bill.'

'Have you phoned Janvier?'

'He'll be here at eight to take over from me.'

'If anyone asks for me, I'll be upstairs . . . Tell the switchboard that all calls are to be put through directly to me . . .'

He did not feel sleepy but did feel sluggish, and his movements were slower than usual. He climbed a narrow staircase which was out of bounds to the public. It led him to the attics of the Palais de Justice. He half opened a door with frosted glass panels and, observing Moers hunched over his instruments, continued on his way as far as Records.

Even before he could open his mouth to speak, the fingerprint expert had given a negative shake of his head.

'Nothing, sir . . .'

In other words, Nine's husband had never been in trouble with the law.

Maigret walked out of the card-index library and went back to see Moers. He took off his overcoat and, after a moment's hesitation, removed his tie, which was too tight around his neck.

The dead man was not here, yet his presence was just as strong as it was in the corpse stored in the racks of the Forensic Institute – drawer 17 – where the mortuary assistant had put him.

No one spoke much . . . Everyone got on with their own work without even noticing that a sliver of sunshine was slanting in through the attic window. In one corner stood an articulated manikin which Maigret had often used before and now used again. Moers, who had had time to give the clothes a good shaking in their various waxed paper bags, was at work analysing the fragments which he had collected in this way.

Maigret meanwhile busied himself with the clothes. With the careful gestures of a window-dresser, starting with the shirt and underpants, he began to dress the manikin, which was about the same size as the dead man.

He had just put the jacket on it when Janvier walked in, looking fresh as a daisy because he had slept in his own bed and had not got up until day was breaking.

'So they got him, sir.'

He looked round for Moers and gave him a wink, which meant that Maigret was not in a chatty mood.

'There's been a report of another yellow car. Lucas, who looked into it, says it's not ours. In any case the number plate ends in nine, not eight.'

Maigret took a step back, to get a view of his handiwork.

'See anything odd?' he asked.

'Wait a moment . . . No . . . I can't see . . . The man was a bit smaller than the manikin. The jacket looks too short . . .'

'That all?'

'The slit made by the knife isn't very wide.'

'Nothing else?'

'He wasn't wearing a waistcoat.'

'What strikes me is that the jacket isn't made of the same cloth as the trousers and isn't the same shade.'

'That happens, you know.'

'But hold on a minute. Take a close look at the trousers. They're virtually new. They're part of a suit. This jacket is part of another suit but is at least two years old.'

'It certainly seems like it.'

'Now the man was quite dapper if his socks, shirt and tie are anything to go by . . . Phone the Caves du Beaujolais and the other bars. Try to find out if yesterday he was wearing a jacket and a pair of trousers which didn't match.'

Janvier sat himself down in a corner. His voice formed a kind of background noise in the lab. He called the bars one by one and repeated time after time:

'It's the Police Judiciaire, the inspector you talked to yesterday . . . Could you tell me if . . .'

Unfortunately, the man had not taken his raincoat off anywhere. He may have unbuttoned it, but no one had paid any attention to the colour of his jacket.

'What do you do when you get home?'

Janvier, who had been married for only a year, answered with a knowing smile:

'I give my wife a kiss . . .'

'After that?'

'I sit down and she brings me my slippers.'

'After that?'

Janvier thought a moment and then hit his forehead with the heel of his hand.

'Got it! I change my jacket!'

'Do you keep a jacket to wear in the house?'

'No. But I put an old one on that I feel more comfortable in.'

And with these words they caught a glimpse of the private life of this unidentified man. They could picture him arriving home and perhaps, like Janvier, kissing his wife, or if not just taking his jacket off and putting on an old one. Then he would eat.

'What's today?'

'Thursday.'

'So yesterday was Wednesday. How often do you eat out? In inexpensive restaurants, the kind where our man would have gone?'

As he spoke, Maigret slipped the beige raincoat over the shoulders of the manikin. Yesterday evening, at about this time, certainly not much later, this gaberdine was still on the back of a living, breathing man who walked into the

Caves du Beaujolais, which was just across the way, virtually under their noses; they had only to look out through the skylight at the opposite bank of the Seine to see it.

He was calling Maigret. He was not asking to speak to just any chief inspector or an inspector or, like those who consider their case to be very important, the commissioner of the Police Judiciaire.

It was Maigret he wanted.

But he had admitted: 'You don't know me . . .'

All the same he had added: 'You used to know my wife, Nine.'

Janvier was wondering what his boss was driving at with all this talk of restaurants.

'Do you like fish pie?'

'I love it. It gives me indigestion, but I eat it whenever I get the chance.'

'Right! Does your wife make it often?'

'No. It's too much bother. It's a dish people don't often make at home.'

'So you have it in restaurants whenever it's on the menu . . .'

'Yes . . .'

'And do you find it on menus very often?'

'I don't know really . . . Let me see . . . Sometimes on a Friday.'

'And yesterday was Wednesday. Get me Dr Paul on the phone.'

The doctor, who was writing up his report, was not surprised by Maigret's question.

'Could you tell me if there were truffles in the fish pie?'

'Absolutely not . . . I would have found fragments . . .'

'Thanks for your help. See, Janvier? There weren't any truffles in the fish pie! That eliminates expensive restaurants, which usually include them. I want you to go down to the inspectors' room. You can get Torrence and two or three others to give you a hand. The switchboard won't like it one bit because you'll be using all their lines for some time. Call all the restaurants one after the other, starting with those located in the parts of town where you were making inquiries yesterday. Find out if any of them had fish pie on their menu last night . . . Wait . . . Try the ones with names having some connection with the south of France first. You're more likely to have luck with them.'

Off Janvier went, not feeling either proud of or overjoyed with the job he had just been landed with.

'Have you got a knife, Moers?'

The morning was wearing on, and Maigret still had not given up on his dead man.

'Slide the point of the blade into the slit in the raincoat . . . Good . . . Now don't move . . .'

He lifted the material slightly so that he could see the jacket underneath.

'The holes in the clothes don't line up . . . Now try angling the blade differently . . . A little more to the left . . . Now to the right . . . Try higher . . . And now lower . . .'

'I get your drift.'

Some of the forensic experts and technicians who were at work in the enormous lab looked on curiously and exchanged amused glances.

'They still don't line up. There's a gap of a good five centimetres between the cut in the jacket and the one in the gaberdine . . . Bring me a chair . . . Give me a hand . . .'

They sat the manikin down, a manoeuvre that called for careful handling.

'That's it . . . When a man is sitting down, leaning against a table, for example, his overcoat may ride up . . . Try it . . .'

But they failed dismally in their efforts to align the two slits, which logically should have been located one exactly above the other.

'That's it!' exclaimed Maigret, as if he had just solved an intricate mathematical equation.

'You mean that when he was killed he wasn't wearing his raincoat?'

'It's virtually certain.'

'But there's a slit in the raincoat that looks as if it was made with a knife.'

'It was done afterwards, to make it look right. Now no one wears a raincoat in a house or a restaurant. By going to the trouble of doctoring the gaberdine, someone was trying to make us believe that the stabbing took place in the open air.'

'. . . whereas the crime was actually carried out indoors,' said Moers, completing his thought.

'And for the same reason, the same person also took the risk of dumping the body in Place de la Concorde, where the murder was not committed . . .'

He knocked his pipe out on his heel, retrieved his tie,

looked some more at the manikin, which seemed even more alive now that it was seated. From the back or the side, when its featureless, colourless face was invisible, the effect was striking.

'Have you found any leads?'

'Almost nothing so far. I haven't finished. But in the arch of the sole I did find small quantities of some very interesting mud. It's soil impregnated with wine, the sort you might find in the wine cellar of a house in the country where a cask has just been broached.'

'Carry on. Phone me in my office.'

When he went in to see the commissioner he was greeted with:

'Well, Maigret? And how is *your dead man?*'

It was the first time the expression had been used. The head of the Police Judiciaire must have been informed that Maigret had had his claws in the case since two in the morning.

'So they managed to get him after all, eh? I admit that yesterday I was more or less convinced that you were dealing with a practical joker or a lunatic.'

'I didn't see it that way. I believed what he said from the first time he phoned.'

Why was that? Maigret could not have put it into words. It certainly wasn't because the man had asked for his help rather than anyone else's. As he spoke to the commissioner, he allowed his eyes to stray out across the river to the opposite bank, which was in full sunlight.

'The public prosecutor has decided the examining magistrate for this case is to be Coméliau. They'll both be dropping in at the Forensic Institute this morning. Do you intend to join them?'

'What would be the point?'

'At least see Coméliau, or call him. He can be touchy.'

Maigret was quite well aware of this.

'You don't think it was some gangland score being settled?'

'I don't know. I'll find out, though it doesn't feel like it to me. The criminal fraternity aren't in the habit of going to the trouble of hanging their victims out to dry in Place de la Concorde.'

'As you wish. Do whatever you think best. I expect someone will recognize him sooner or later.'

'I'd be surprised.'

This was another feeling which he would have been hard pressed to explain. In his mind, it made perfect sense. But as soon as he tried to pin it down, even for his own satisfaction, the waters grew muddy.

But there was no getting away from Place de la Concorde. It followed that someone wanted the body to be found, and found quickly. It would have been easier and less dangerous, for example, to throw it into the Seine, where it might have remained for days if not weeks before it was fished out.

The victim was not a rich man or a famous person but a nonentity, a man of no importance.

So why, if they wanted the police to get interested in him, rearrange his face after he was dead and empty his pockets of everything which might have been used to identify him?

Still, they hadn't removed the label on the jacket. But that was obviously because they knew that he was wearing ready-made clothes which had been sold by the thousand.

'You look worried, Maigret.'

But all he could do was repeat:

'It doesn't hang together . . .'

Too many details which did not fit. One detail in particular bothered him; it quite upset him, in fact.

At what time had the last phone call been made? As things stood, the last sign of life the man had given was the note handed in at the post office in Faubourg Saint-Denis.

That had happened in the clear light of day. Ever since eleven that morning, the nameless man had not missed any opportunity for making contact with Maigret.

Even in the note, he had been appealing directly to him, and more insistently than ever. He had even asked him to alert officers on duty so that any one of them would have been aware of the situation and been ready to come to his aid in the street at the first sign he gave.

But the fact was that he had been killed between eight and ten in the evening.

What had he been doing between four and eight o'clock? There had been no sign of him, no trace. Just silence, a silence which had struck Maigret the previous evening, even though he had kept his concerns to himself. It had reminded him of a real-life underwater disaster which, as it unfolded, had been followed all over the world minute by minute on the radio. At certain times, listeners had heard the signal sent out by the men entombed in the submarine stranded on the ocean bed and could imagine the rescue vessels circling on the surface. The intervals between signals grew longer. Then suddenly, after many hours: nothing.

But Maigret's unnamed dead man had no valid reason for keeping quiet. He could not have been kidnapped in full daylight in a busy Paris street. And he had not been killed before eight o'clock.

Everything seemed to suggest that he had gone home, because he had changed his jacket.

He had eaten either at home or in a restaurant. And he had been left alone to eat his dinner because he had had enough time to consume soup, fish pie and an apple. Everything up to and including the apple suggested peace and calm.

So why had he not spoken for two hours?

He had not hesitated to pester Maigret several times and urge him to put the whole police force on high alert.

Then suddenly, after four o'clock, it was as if he had changed his mind, as though he had wanted to leave the police out of the reckoning altogether.

It nettled Maigret. That's not the right word perhaps, but it felt a little as if his dead man had been unfaithful to him.

'Got anything, Janvier?'

The inspectors' room was blue with tobacco smoke. Four glassy-eyed men were glued to phones.

'Fish pie's not on the menu, sir!' joked Janvier with a sigh, 'and yet we've covered the primary area. I'm now doing the Faubourg Montmartre, and Torrence has got as far as Place Clichy . . .'

Maigret also got on the phone in his office, but he was calling a small cheap hotel in Rue Lepic.

'Yes, by taxi . . . At once . . .'

Someone had left photos of the dead man on his desk taken during the night. There were also copies of the morning papers, reports and a note from the examining magistrate, Coméliau.

'Is that you, Madame Maigret? . . . Not too bad . . . I don't know yet if I'll be home for lunch . . . No, I haven't had time to get a shave . . . I'll try and get to a barber's . . . Yes, I've eaten . . .'

He duly went out to find a barber's, but not before telling old Joseph, the office clerk, to ask a visitor who would be coming to see him to wait. He did not have far to go, just across the bridge. He walked into the first gentleman's hairdresser's he came to on Boulevard Saint-Michel and stared grimly at the large, dark-ringed eyes which looked back at him from the mirror.

He knew that when he left he would not be able to resist the temptation of going for a drink in the Caves du Beaujolais. First, because he was genuinely fond of the atmosphere in that type of small bar which is generally very quiet and the landlord will pass the time of day with you. He also liked Beaujolais, especially when it is served, as it was there, in those small stoneware mugs. But there was another reason: he was following in the steps of his dead man.

'Reading the paper this morning, inspector, it gave me quite a shock. I didn't see much of him, you know. But when I think about it, he seemed decent enough. I can see him now, waving his arms about as he came in. He was on edge, that's for sure, but he looked a straightforward sort. Know what? I bet he'd have been good fun in other circumstances. You'll laugh, but the more I think about it, the more I think he was a joker. He reminded me of somebody. I been trying to remember who for hours.'

'Somebody that looked like him?'

'Yes . . . No . . . It's more complicated . . . He reminds me of something, and I can't for the life of me remember what . . . Has he been identified yet?'

That too was strange, though not altogether unusual at this stage. The morning editions had been out for some time. Of course, the face was disfigured but not to the point of being unrecognizable to anyone who was close to him, a wife or mother, for example.

The man had lived somewhere, even if it was only a hotel. He hadn't been home all night.

Logically, in the last few hours, someone must have either recognized his photo or reported his disappearance.

But Maigret was not counting on anything. He recrossed the bridge with a pleasant, slightly harsh aftertaste of Beaujolais in his mouth. He climbed the shabby staircase, where eyes watched him with apprehensive respect.

He glanced through the windows of the waiting room. His man was there, on his feet, perfectly at home, smoking a cigarette.

'This way . . .'

He showed him into his office, motioned him to a chair and took off his hat and coat without ceasing to observe his visitor out of the corner of his eye. From where he was, his visitor had a clear view of the photos of the dead man.

'Well, Fred?'

'I'm all yours, inspector. I wasn't expecting you to phone. I don't see how . . .'

He was thin, very pale, and smartly dressed in a vaguely effeminate way. From time to time, a tautening of the nostrils identified a drug addict.

'You don't know him?'

'I knew what this is about when I got here, the minute I saw the photos . . . Looks like someone's beat him up!'

'You never saw him before?'

It was clear that Fred was trying his level best to do what was expected of him as a police informer. He looked closely at the photos and even took them to the window so that he could see them in full light.

'No . . . And yet . . .'

While Maigret waited, he refilled the stove.

'It's no go! I'd swear I never saw him before. But he puts me in mind of something. I can't put my finger on it . . . But at any rate he's not part of any mob. Even if he was a new recruit I'd have come across him already.'

'What does he remind you of?'

'That's exactly what I'm trying to remember . . . Do you know what line of work he was in?'

'No.'

'Nor what part of Paris he lived in?'

'No.'

'He's not from out of town either, you can tell straight off.'

'I agree.'

Maigret had had ample opportunity to hear for himself that the man had a marked Parisian accent, the lower-class accent heard everywhere, on the Métro, in the bars on the outskirts and also in the stands of the Vélodrome d'Hiver.

Actually . . . He had the beginnings of an idea . . . He would test it later . . .

'I don't suppose you know a woman named Nine either?'

'Wait a sec . . . There's a Nine in Marseilles, plays second fiddle to the madam of a brothel in Rue Saint-Ferréol.'

'It's not her, I know that one . . . She's at least fifty years old . . .'

Fred stared at the photo of the man who was probably about thirty and muttered:

'It doesn't always follow, you know!'

'Take one of these photos. Try to remember. Show it round . . .'

'You can count on me. I hope I'll have a lead for you within a couple of days. Not about your stiff, but about a big-time drugs dealer. For now I only know him as Monsieur Jean. I've never seen him. All I know is that he's behind a big gang of small-fry dealers. I get my stuff from them regularly. It costs me. When you've got some cash to spare . . .'

Next door, Janvier was still on the trail of fish pie.

'You're right, sir. Everyone I talk to says they only make Provençal fish pie on Fridays, and even then, not that often. During Holy Week, sometimes on a Wednesday, but Easter is still a long way off.'

'Leave that to Torrence. Is there anything on at the Vél' d'Hiv' this afternoon?'

'Wait a minute, I'll look in the paper.'

There were motor-paced races.

'Take a photo along with you. Talk to the ticket offices, orange sellers and peanut vendors. Tour all the bars in the area. Then hang about in the cafés around Porte Dauphine.'

'You think he was a sporting type?'

Maigret had no idea. He had a feeling too, just like the others, like the landlord of the Caves du Beaujolais, like the informer Fred, but it was unfocused, blurred.

He could not picture his dead man working in an office or as a shop assistant. Fred had been definite that he was not part of the criminal underworld.

On the other hand, he was completely at home in small working-class bars.

He had a wife called Nine. And Maigret had met her. In what capacity? Would the man have made a point of mentioning it if the inspector had encountered her as someone he had investigated?

'Come here, Dubonnet. I want you to go down to Vice. Ask to see the list of girls who've been registered over the last few years. Note down the addresses of all the ones named Nine. Then go and see them. Is that clear?'

Dubonnet was a young officer, fresh out of college, a little stiff, always very well turned out, exquisitely courteous to all and sundry. It was perhaps Maigret's sense of irony which had made him choose him for the job.

He sent another inspector to make inquiries in all the small bars around Châtelet, Place des Vosges and Bastille.

Meanwhile, Coméliau, the examining magistrate, who was leading the investigation from his office, waited impatiently for Maigret. He did not understand why he had not already contacted him.

'What about the yellow Citroëns?'

'Ériau is looking after it.'

All that was routine. But even if it served no purpose, it had to be done. On all the roads in France, policemen and uniformed officers were pulling over all drivers of yellow Citroëns.

Someone also had to be sent to the shop on Boulevard Sébastopol where the dead man's jacket had been bought, and also to another establishment on Boulevard Saint-Martin where the raincoat had been sold.

While that was proceeding, fifty other cases were demanding the attention of the inspectors. They came in, went out, phoned, typed up reports . . . People were kept waiting in the corridors. There was a deal of toing and froing between the Hotel Agency and Vice Squad and between Vice and Records.

Moers' voice over the phone:

'Maybe something, sir . . . A small detail, which is probably not important. I've found so little that I'll bring it to your attention anyway. I took a hair sample, as usual. My analysis revealed traces of lipstick.'

It was almost laughable, but neither of them was laughing. A woman had kissed Maigret's dead man on the head, a woman wearing lipstick.

'I can add that it's a cheap make, and that the woman is probably a brunette, because it's a dark shade of red . . .'

Was it the previous evening that a woman had kissed the man with no name? Did it happen at his place when he had gone home to change his jacket?

And since he had actually changed, it was because he wasn't intending to go out again. A man who goes home for just an hour does not bother to put on a different jacket.

In which case, then, he had been called away unexpectedly . . . But was it likely that, hunted as he was and sufficiently panicky to go running around Paris waving his arms about and phoning the police all day, he would have gone out after dark?

A woman kissed his hair. Or else she had bent over him, leaning her face against his cheek. Either way it was a tender gesture.

Maigret sighed, filled his pipe again and looked at the clock. It was a few minutes after midday.

Almost exactly the same time as when, on the previous day, the man had walked across Place des Vosges while the fountains played.

Maigret went through the small communicating door which connected the Police Judiciaire with the Palais de Justice. Lawyers' robes billowed in the corridors like great black birds.

'Let's go and see the old baboon!' sighed Maigret who had never been able to stand Coméliau.

He knew in advance that the examining magistrate would greet him with some icy comment which in his eyes would be the most stinging rebuke he could think of:

'Ah! I have been waiting for you, Detective Chief Inspector . . .'

Though he would have been quite capable of saying,
like Louis XIV:

'I almost had to wait . . .'

Maigret could not have cared less.

He had been living with his dead man since half past
two that morning.

3.

'I am delighted, Maigret, to have got you on the phone at long last.'

'Believe me, sir, the pleasure is all mine.'

Madame Maigret looked up sharply. She always felt uneasy when her husband used that quiet, bland voice. When he used it on her she always cried because she never knew what was coming next.

'I've called you at your office five times.'

'And I wasn't there!' he sighed, audibly dismayed.

She raised a finger, warning him to be careful and remember that he was speaking to an examining magistrate who moreover had a brother-in-law who had been a government minister two or three times.

'I've only just been told that you were unwell.'

'A little off colour, sir. People always exaggerate these things. A heavy cold. And I wonder now if it really was as heavy as all that!'

It was perhaps the fact that he was at home, in his pyjamas and wearing his velvety dressing gown, his feet encased in slippers and comfortably settled in his armchair, that put him in such a playful mood.

'What surprises me is that you haven't let me know who is replacing you.'

'Replacing me where?'

Coméliau's voice was curt, cool, deliberately impersonal, whereas Maigret's became increasingly amenable.

'I'm talking about the Place de la Concorde murder. I assume you haven't forgotten it?'

'It is constantly in my thoughts. Why, only this minute I was telling my wife . . .'

But she made even more emphatic signs ordering him not to involve her in the affair. Their apartment was small and cosy. The furniture in the dining room was all dark oak and dated from the time of Maigret's marriage. Opposite, through the net curtains, could be seen in large black letters on a white wall: 'Lhoste & Pépin – Makers of Precision Tools'.

Every morning and every evening for thirty years, Maigret had been seeing those words, and under them the huge warehouse doors and two or three lorries branded with the same names eternally parked on either side of them, and he was still not sick of the view.

On the contrary! He liked it. He would let his eyes linger on it, almost lovingly. Then without fail he would raise them to the rear of a distant house, where washing was put out of the windows to dry and a red geranium would appear in one of them as soon as the weather turned warm enough.

It was probably not the same geranium. He would have sworn, however, that the same flower pot had been there, as he had, for the last thirty years. And during all that time not once had Maigret ever seen anyone lean on the sill and look out or water the plant. Obviously someone lived in that room, but his or her hours could never have coincided with his.

'Are you sure, Monsieur Maigret, that in your absence your subordinates are conducting the inquiry with the necessary zeal?'

'I believe so, Monsieur Coméliau. Indeed, I am certain of it. You cannot imagine how helpful it is, when directing an investigation of this sort, to be in a quiet, overheated room, sitting in an armchair in one's own home, far from all the usual distractions, with nothing but a phone within easy reach and a pot of herbal tea to hand. I will let you in on a little secret: I'm wondering, if this case had not cropped up, if I would have been feeling unwell at all. Obviously I wouldn't be ill since it was in Place de la Concorde on the night the body was discovered that I caught cold. Or perhaps it was early that morning, while Dr Paul and I walked along the bank of the river at first light, after the autopsy. But that isn't what I mean. If it hadn't been for this investigation, my cold would have been just a cold and I would have ignored it. Do you see what I'm getting at?'

In his office, Coméliau's face had probably turned yellow, possibly green, and poor Madame Maigret, who had such respect for rank and hierarchies of all kinds, did not know where to put herself.

'So let's just say that, that I have much more peace here, at home, with my wife looking after me, to think about the case and manage it. I'm not disturbed by anyone, or hardly anyone . . .'

'Maigret!' chided his wife.

'Sh!'

Coméliau was speaking.

'You think it usual that after three days the man still has not been identified? His picture has been in all the papers. I understand from what you told me that there was a wife.'

'Indeed so, he told me himself.'

'Please let me speak. He had a wife and probably friends. He also had neighbours, a landlord and so on and so forth. People were used to seeing him walking along the street at certain times. But no one so far has come forward to identify him or report his disappearance. Still, not everyone knows how to get to Boulevard Richard-Lenoir.'

Poor Boulevard Richard-Lenoir! Why on earth should it have such a bad name? Obviously, it led into Place de la Bastille. Equally obviously it was flanked on both sides by narrow, teeming streets. And the area was full of small workshops and warehouses. But the Boulevard itself was wide and even had a grassy central reservation. Admittedly, the grass grew above the Métro line, and here and there air-vents exhaled warm fumes which smelled of disinfectant, and every couple of minutes when trains trundled by underneath the houses shook in the most curious way. But people were used to it. Many times over the last thirty years, friends and colleagues had found other apartments for him in what they called more 'vibrant' parts of town. He would go to see them and mutter:

'It's very nice, I see that . . .'

'But what about the view, Maigret?'

'Yes . . .'

'The rooms are big and airy . . .'

'Agreed . . . It's perfect . . . I'd really like living here . . . But . . .'

He would take his time before saying with a sigh and a regretful shake of his head:

'. . . I'd have to move!'

It was just hard luck on people who didn't care for Boulevard Richard-Lenoir. And too bad for Coméliau.

'Tell me, sir, did you ever happen to push a dried pea up your nose?'

'I beg your pardon?'

'A dried pea. I remember we used to play at doing it when I was a boy. Try it. Then look at yourself in a mirror. You'll be surprised by the result. I'd bet that with a dried pea in one of your nostrils you could walk past people who see you every day without them recognizing you. Nothing alters the cast of a face more. And those who are most accustomed to seeing us are the ones who are the most disconcerted by the smallest change.

'But as you are aware, our man's face was rearranged much more severely than by a pea up his nose.

'And there's something else. It's hard for people to imagine that their next-door neighbour, someone they work with in the office or the waiter who serves them every lunchtime can suddenly become different from what they always are and turn, for example, into a murderer or a corpse. People learn about crime through newspapers and come to think that such things happen in another world, another part of the wood entirely. Not on *their* street. Not in *their* apartment block.'

'So, broadly speaking, you don't think it unusual that no one has identified him yet?'

'I am not unduly surprised. I remember the case of a woman who had drowned, and with her it took six months. And that was in the days of the old morgue before refrigeration came in, and the bodies just had a trickle of cold water running over them from a tap!'

Madame Maigret sighed, abandoning all thought of trying to shut him up.

'So in a word you are quite happy with the way things stand. A man is killed, and after three days not only is there no trace of the murderer but we don't know anything about the victim!'

'I know lots of small things about him, sir.'

'So small, it seems, that they aren't deemed worthy of being passed on to me, even though I am in charge of this investigation.'

'All right, here's an example. The man was a smart dresser. Though his taste was dubious, he gave much thought to his appearance, as we can tell by his socks and tie. Also, with grey trousers and a gaberdine raincoat he wore black kid shoes and expensively fine socks.'

'Really? How interesting.'

'Very interesting, especially since he was also wearing a white shirt. Now wouldn't you have thought that a man who liked mauve socks and floral ties would have preferred a coloured shirt, or at least one with stripes or a small pattern? Walk into any bar like the ones he led us to, where he seemed very much at home, and you won't see many plain white shirts.'

'What's your point?'

'Give me a moment. In at least two of those bars – Torrence went back and asked – he ordered a Suze and lemon, as it seems he always did.'

'So we know what kind of aperitif he liked!'

'Have you ever drunk Suze, sir? Gentian bitters? It has an astringent taste and is not very alcoholic. It's not the kind of aperitif that's served just anywhere. I also have noticed that people who order Suze are not often the ones who go to cafés for the lift you get from a pre-dinner drink but men who patronize such establishments for professional reasons, like commercial travellers who are obliged to accept lots of free drinks.'

'So you deduce from this that the dead man was a commercial traveller?'

'No.'

'What, then?'

'Hear me out. Five or six people saw him and we have their statements. None of them could give us a detailed description. Most of them speak of a small-made, ordinary man who waved his arms about. I was forgetting one detail which Moers came up with this morning. He is very conscientious, never satisfied with his work. He goes back and checks without being asked to. Well, he's discovered that the dead man walked like a duck.'

'How do you mean?'

'Like a duck! With his feet pointing out, if you prefer.'

He gestured to Madame Maigret, indicating that she should fill his pipe. He watched her out of the corner of his eye, using his hands to stop her packing the bowl too tightly.

'I was telling you about the various descriptions we have of him. They are vague. Even so, two out of the five had the same impression. "I'm not sure," said the owner of the Caves du Beaujolais. "I can't say exactly . . . But he reminds me of something . . . But what?" Now he wasn't a film actor. He wasn't even an extra. An inspector asked around all the studios. Nor was he a politician or a magistrate . . .'

'Maigret!' cried his wife.

Still talking, he lit his pipe, punctuating his flow with pulls on his pipe.

'Ask yourself, sir, what profession matches up with all these details.'

'I don't care for charades.'

'When a man is forced to keep to his room, you know, he has plenty of time for reflection. But I'm forgetting the most important thing. Of course, we looked at various spheres of activity. Cycle races and football matches drew blanks. I had all PMU licensees questioned . . .'

'All what?'

'The Pari-Mutuel-Urbain . . . You've seen cafés where you can put a bet on a horse without having to go to the races. I don't know why, but I saw my man as the sort who'd hang around PMU bars. But that didn't turn up anything either . . .'

He had the patience of an angel. It was as if he relished spinning this phone call out for as long as he could.

'On the other hand, Lucas had more luck at the races. It took him some time. We're not talking about a formal identification. The disfigurement of the face remains a problem. And don't forget either that people aren't used to seeing dead bodies, only living people, plus the fact that when a man becomes a corpse he changes his appearance greatly . . . Still, on race tracks, a few people remember him . . . He wasn't a habitué of the paddock but of the public enclosures. According to one tipster, he was something of a regular.'

'But all this has still not been enough to reveal his identity?'

'No. But this plus the rest, everything I've told you, allows me to say almost for sure that he was in La Limonade . . .'

'La Limonade?''

'It's the usual term, sir. It covers waiters, bottle-washers, bartenders and even some café owners. It's the word used in the trade for everyone who works in the drinks industry but excludes restaurants. Now all waiters in bars are the same. I don't mean that they all look exactly the same, but there's a family likeness. How often does it happen that you have the feeling that you recognize a waiter you've never actually seen before?'

'Most of them have sensitive feet, as you would expect. You only have to look at their feet. They wear light, supple shoes, almost like slippers. You'll never see a waiter in a bar or a head waiter in a restaurant wearing outdoor shoes, with triple soles. And their profession requires them to wear white shirts.

'I'm not saying that it's compulsory, but there is also a fair percentage who walk like ducks.

'I would also add that, for reasons which escape me,

waiters who work in bars have a pronounced weakness for horse-racing and that many of those who work early or late shifts, are keen race-goers.'

'So, to get to the point, you have come to the conclusion that our man was a waiter in a café.'

'No, actually.'

'Then I don't understand.'

'He was part of the lemonade club but not a waiter. I've given it hours of thought as I lay here dozing.'

Each word, sculpted in ice, must have shaken Coméliau.

'Everything I've told you about waiters also applies to bar-owners. Don't think I'm boasting but I always felt that my dead man wasn't an employee but rather someone who worked for himself. That is why, at eleven this morning, I phoned Moers. The shirt is still with Criminal Records. I couldn't remember what state it was in. He had another look at it. Here, luck was on our side because it could have been brand new. Everyone puts on a new shirt from time to time. Fortunately, this one wasn't. It is quite worn round the collar.'

'Are you going to tell me that the owners of bars wear out their shirts at the collar?'

'No, sir. Not more than anyone else.

'But they don't wear them out at the wrists. I'm talking about small cafés with a lower-class clientele, not the American-style bars around the Opera House or on the Champs-Élysées. The owners of small bars who have their hands continually in water or ice keep their sleeves rolled up all the time. Now, Moers confirmed that the shirt, worn at the collar to the point where it had been rubbed threadbare, shows no trace of wear on the cuffs.'

What was beginning to unsettle Madame Maigret was the way he was now speaking with deep conviction.

'And when you add the fish pie . . .'

'Is a taste for it also particular to the owners of small bars?'

'No, sir. But Paris is full of little bars which serve food for a small number of customers. You know: no tablecloth, they eat directly off the table. Often it's the owner's wife who does the cooking. The menu consists of the dish of the day and nothing else. In such bars, where there are quiet periods, the owner is free for a good part of the afternoon. That's why this morning I've got two inspectors trawling through every part of Paris, starting with the area round the Hôtel de Ville and Bastille. As you know, our man never strayed very far from there. Parisians are fiercely attached to their own neighbourhood because it's probably only there that they feel really safe.'

'Are you hoping for a result soon?'

'I hope there'll be a positive result sooner or later. Now let me see . . . Have I told you everything? All I have left to report is the spot of varnish.'

'What varnish?'

'On the seat of the trousers. It was Moers – who else? – who spotted it, though it's visible enough. He reckons it's fresh varnish. He also says the varnish was applied to some piece of furniture three or four days ago. I've sent men out to the mainline stations, starting with Gare de Lyon.'

'Why Gare de Lyon?'

'Because it's a kind of extension of the Bastille district.'

'And why start in a station?'

Maigret sighed. Oh God! How long it took to explain things! How could an examining magistrate be so deficient in even the most basic sense of the common realities! How can people who have never set foot in a cheap bar, or a PMU café or in the public enclosures of a race-course, how can such people, who don't know the meaning of the expression *Limonade*, claim to be capable of understanding the criminal mind?

'I assume you have my report there?'

'I've read it several times.'

'When I got the first phone call on Wednesday morning at eleven, the man had had someone tailing him for some time, since the previous evening, at least. He didn't think of contacting the police immediately. He clearly hoped he'd be able to sort his problem out himself. Yet he was already scared. He knew they wanted to kill him. So he had to avoid places where there weren't any people. The crowd was his shield. Nor did he dare go home, where they would have followed him and finished him off. Now, even in Paris there are very few places that stay open all night. In addition to the Montmartre nightclubs, there are the railway stations, which are lit and have waiting rooms that are never empty. Well, it so happens that the benches in the third-class waiting room at Gare de Lyon were re-varnished on Monday. Moers confirms that the varnish used there is identical to the one on the trousers.'

'Have the station staff been questioned?'

'Yes, and they are still being interviewed, sir.'

'In short, then, you have managed despite the difficulties to get some results.'

'Despite the difficulties, yes. I also know exactly when our man changed his mind.'

'Changed his mind about what?'

Madame Maigret was pouring her husband a cup of herbal tea and made signs telling him to drink it while it was hot.

'First, as I've just explained, he hoped to sort out his problem by himself. Then, on Wednesday morning he got the idea of contacting me. He persisted with that idea until about four in the afternoon. What happened then? I don't know. Perhaps, after sending out his last SOS from the post office in Faubourg Saint-Denis, he decided he wasn't getting anywhere? Be that as it may, but about an hour later, around five, he walked into a bar in Rue Saint-Antoine.'

'So a witness has come forward at last?'

'No, sir. It was Janvier who came up with it after showing the photo in all the bars and questioning waiters. Anyway, he ordered a Suze – and this fact virtually rules out any chance that we've got the wrong man – and asked for an envelope. Not writing paper, just an envelope. Then he stuffed it in his pocket, asked at the counter for a token for the phone and hurried into the booth. He made a call. The woman at the till heard the click of the receiver.'

'And you did not get that call?'

'No,' said Maigret with a touch of resentment. 'It wasn't

meant for us. It was intended for someone else, obviously. As for the yellow car . . .'

'Any news of it?'

'What there is is vague though consistent. Are you familiar with Quai Henri-IV?'

'Near the Bastille?'

'That's right. As you see, everything happens within the same area, so much so that you get the feeling that you're going round and round in circles. Now, Quai Henri-IV is one of the quietest and least frequented parts of Paris. There's not a single shop, not one bar, just well-heeled, residential streets. A telegram delivery boy spotted the yellow car at eight exactly. He noticed it because it had broken down outside number 63, where he happened to have a telegram to deliver. Two men had their heads under the raised bonnet.'

'Was he able to give you a description?'

'No, it was too dark.'

'Did he get the number?'

'No again. It is rare, sir, that it crosses anyone's mind to make a note of the registration numbers of cars they happen to notice. But what is important is that the car was facing towards Pont d'Austerlitz. Also it was then ten past eight, which is significant given that we know from the autopsy that the murder was committed between eight and ten.'

'Do you think your health will allow you to get out and about again soon?'

The tone of the examining magistrate had softened slightly, but he was in no mood to make concessions.

'I don't know.'

'In what direction are you now pursuing your inquiries?'

'No particular direction. I'm waiting. That's all I can do, wouldn't you agree? We've come to a standstill. We've done, or rather my men have done, all we could. All we can do now is wait.'

'Wait for what?'

'Anything. Whatever turns up. Maybe a witness? A new fact?'

'Do you think that will happen?'

'We have to hope so.'

'Well, thank you for all this. I shall forward a report of our conversation to the public prosecutor.'

'Please convey my best wishes to him.'

'I hope your health picks up.'

'Thank you.'

As he replaced the receiver, he looked as grave as an owl. Out of the corner of his eye, he observed Madame Maigret, who had taken up her knitting again and, he sensed, was feeling vaguely concerned.

'Don't you think you went a little too far?'

'Too far in what direction?'

'Admit it: you were having him on.'

'Not at all.'

'But you kept making fun of him.'

'Do you think so?'

He seemed genuinely surprised. Indeed, the truth was that, for all his banter, he had been deadly serious. Everything he had said was true, including the doubts he had about his state of health. This happened to him from time to time, out of the blue, when an investigation was not moving forwards the way he would like: he would take to his bed or stay in his room. He would then be pampered, and everyone would walk by on tiptoe. This way he escaped from the bustle and hubbub of the Police Judiciaire, from the questions fired at him from left and right, the countless daily irritations. But now colleagues came to visit him or phoned him up. Everyone was patient with him. They kept asking him how he was. And in exchange for a few cups of herbal tea, which he drank with sulky bad grace, he managed to extract a few grogs from the ever solicitous Madame Maigret.

It was true that he had various things in common with his dead man. Fundamentally – the thought suddenly crossed his mind – it was not so much the business of moving house that alarmed him but the fact that he would moving to fresh pastures, the prospect of not seeing the words 'Lhoste & Pépin' when he woke and of not following the same route every morning, normally on foot. The dead man and he were both solidly rooted in their settings. It was a thought that pleased him. He emptied his pipe and filled another.

'Do you really think he's the proprietor of a bar?'

'I may have exaggerated slightly by being so definite, but I said it and would like it to be true. It all holds together, don't you see?'

'What holds together?'

'Everything I told him. At the start, I didn't think I'd tell him as much as I did. I was thinking out loud. But then I felt that it was all coming together. So I carried on.'

'And what if he was a cobbler or a tailor?'

'Dr Paul would have told me. Moers too.'

'How would they have known?'

'Dr Paul would have known by studying the hands, the calluses and any tell-tale signs; Moers by analysing the particles found in his clothes.'

'And what if it turns out that he was anything but a man who ran a bar?'

'It would be just too bad. Pass me my book.'

That was another of his habits when he was not feeling well: to lose himself in a novel by Alexandre Dumas *père*. He owned a set of his complete works in an old, cheap edition with yellowing pages and romantic engravings. The mere smell of those volumes brought back memories of all the times when he had been briefly laid up.

There was the muted purr of the stove as it drew and the click of knitting needles. Whenever he looked up he saw the brass pendulum swinging in its dark oak case.

'You should take some more aspirins.'

'As you wish.'

'Why do you think he phoned someone else?'

Loyal Madame Maigret! She would so much have liked to help him. Usually, she consciously refrained from asking questions about his work, even about the time he would be home and when he wanted his meals. But when he was ill and she saw him working, she could not help worrying. Basically, deep down, she probably thought he was not taking it seriously.

On the other hand, when he was at the Police Judiciaire, he probably behaved differently and acted and spoke like a real detective chief inspector.

This discussion he had just had with Coméliau – especially because of who he was – had been torture for her, and it was obvious that even as she counted her stitches she was still thinking about it.

'Listen, Maigret . . .'

He looked up reluctantly, for he was deep in his book.

'There's something I don't understand. You said when you were talking about Gare de Lyon that he didn't dare go home because the man would have followed him.'

'Yes, I probably said that.'

'Yesterday, you told me he'd changed his jacket.'

'True. What about it?'

'And you've just told Monsieur Coméliau about the fish pie, implying that he'd eaten it in his own restaurant. So he did go back. Therefore he wasn't afraid of being followed home.'

Had Maigret really had this thought already? Or on the contrary, was he improvising when he replied?

'There's no contradiction.'

'Oh.'

'The station episode was Tuesday evening. It was before he had contacted me. He was still hoping he'd be able to escape from the man who was following him.'

'What about the next day? Do you think he wasn't being followed any more?'

'Maybe yes. It's more than likely. But I also said that he changed his mind, around five o'clock. Don't forget he phoned somebody and asked for an envelope.'

'That's true.'

Although she was not convinced, she thought it wise to answer with a sigh:

'You're probably right.'

Then there was silence. From time to time a page turned, and the sock in Madame Maigret's lap grew longer in tiny increments.

She opened her mouth, then closed it. Without looking up, he said:

'Out with it!'

'It's nothing . . . . It surely doesn't mean anything . . . Only I was just thinking that he got it wrong since he was killed in the end . . .'

'Where did he go wrong?'

'About going home. I'm sorry. Read your book . . .'

But he didn't read, at least not very attentively, because it was he who looked up first.

'You're forgetting the car that broke down,' he said.

And he felt that a new avenue had suddenly opened up for his thoughts, that a curtain had been whisked aside and that beyond it he would glimpse the truth.

'What we need to know is how long exactly it was before the yellow car was repaired.'

He had ceased speaking for her benefit. She knew it and made sure she didn't interrupt him again.

'A car breakdown is an unpredictable event. It is an accident, something which by definition upsets the most carefully made schemes. It follows that events turned out to be different from what had been planned.'

He gave his wife a shrewd look: it was she who had set him on the right path.

'*Suppose he died because the car had broken down?*'

Without further ado he slammed the book shut and left it on his knees. Then he reached for the phone and dialled the number of the Police Judiciaire.

'Give me Lucas. If he's not in his office, he'll be in mine . . . Is that you, Lucas? . . . What? . . . There's been a development? . . . Wait a moment . . .'

He wanted to say his piece first: he was afraid he would be told what he had worked out for himself.

'I want you to send a man out to Quai Henri-IV, Ériau or Dubonnet, if they're available. I want him to question all the concierges, all the tenants not only of number 63 and the immediately neighbouring houses but also in all the houses and apartments. The street isn't very long. Some of the locals must have noticed the yellow car, and I'd like to know, as accurately as possible, exactly when it broke down and what time it drove away again. Wait! That's not all! The men in the car might have wanted a spare part. There must be garages in the area. I want them questioned too. That's all for the moment . . . over to you!'

'One moment, sir, I have to go next door . . .'

That meant that Lucas was not alone and that he did not want to speak in front of the person who was with him.

'Hello? . . . Right . . . I didn't want her to hear what I was saying. It's further information about the car. An old lady turned up half an hour ago, and I'm interviewing her in your office. Unfortunately, she seems a bit crazy to me . . .'

It was unavoidable. However little publicity is given to a police investigation, the Police Judiciaire sooner or later attracts all the crazy people, male and female, in Paris.

'She lives on Quai de Charenton, a little further along than the warehouses at Bercy.'

It reminded Maigret of a case he had investigated a few years before in a strange little house located in that part of the city. In his mind's eye, he saw Quai de Bercy, with the warehouse gates on the left, the tall trees and the stone parapet of the Seine on the right. Further on, after a bridge whose name he had forgotten, the road widened. One side was lined with one- or two- storied houses which put him in mind more of the suburbs than of the inner city proper. There were always many barges moored just there, and he pictured the docks piled high with barrels as far as the eye could see.

'What does this old woman do for a living?'

'That's the hitch. She's a fortune-teller and clairvoyant . . .'

'Oh dear.'

'That was my first reaction too. She talks the hind leg off a donkey and she has this very unnerving way of looking at you straight in the eye. At first, she stated categorically that she never reads newspapers and tried to make me believe that there was no point because she only had to go into a trance to be up to date with everything that goes on.'

'You pressed her?'

'Yes. In the end she admitted that she might just have glanced at a paper which one of her customers had left behind.'

'So?'

'She'd read a description of the yellow car. She claims she saw it on Wednesday evening less than a hundred metres from her front door.'

'What time was that?'

'About nine.'

'Did she see who was in it?'

'She saw two men going into a building.'

'And is she able to say which building?'

'It's a small bar on the corner of the Quai and a street that runs off it. It's called the Petit Albert.'

Maigret bit hard on the pipe between his teeth and avoided looking at Madame Maigret, for he was reluctant to let her see the tiny flame dancing in his eyes.

'Is that all?'

'That's more or less everything interesting that she told me. But that didn't stop her yakking on and on for half an hour at an alarming rate. Would it be better if you talked to her?'

'Yes!'

'Would you like me to bring her round to your place?'

'Just a moment. Do we know how long the car remained outside the Petit Albert?'

'About half an hour.'

'And it drove off towards the centre of town?'

'No. It headed along the river bank towards Charenton.'

'Was any kind of parcel transferred from the building to the car? Do you see what I'm getting at?'

'No, nothing. She reckons that the men weren't carrying anything. And that's what puzzles me. There's also the time factor. I'm wondering what the men could have done with the body between nine that night and one in the morning. They can't have just gone driving around the countryside. Shall I bring the old woman round now?'

'Yes. Get a taxi and hang on to it. Bring an inspector with you. He can wait downstairs with the old woman.'

'You're going to leave your house?'

'Yes.'

'But what about your bronchitis?'

It was kind of Lucas: he said 'bronchitis' instead of 'cold', which made it sound more serious.

'Don't you worry about that.'

Madame Maigret began stirring on her chair and almost said something.

'Tell the inspector not to let her run off while you're coming up the stairs. Some people get sudden urges to change their minds.'

'I don't think she's one of them. She's keen to see her photo in the papers along with all her titles and qualifications. She wanted to know where the photographers were.'

'Well, have her photographed before you leave. She'll like having her picture taken.'

He hung up, gave Madame Maigret a look full of gentle irony then lowered his eyes to his Alexandre Dumas, which he hadn't finished and probably wouldn't finish this time round. It would have to wait until he was ill on some other occasion. He also spared a glance, but one of disdain, for the cup of herbal tea.

'To work!' he exclaimed as he stood up and made straight for the cupboard, from which he produced the decanter of calvados and a liqueur glass with a gilt rim.

'It was worth filling you full of aspirin so that you would sweat it out!'

4.

In the annals of the Police Judiciaire are a number of 'stake-outs' which are invariably trotted out for the benefit of new recruits. Among them is one of Maigret's, now fifteen years old. It was late autumn, at the very worst time of year, especially in Normandy, where the low, leaden sky makes the days even shorter. For three days and two nights, Maigret had remained outside the garden gate on a deserted road on the outskirts of Fécamp, waiting for a man to emerge from the house opposite. There were no other houses in sight, only fields. Even the cows were under cover. To ask to be relieved, he would have had to walk two kilometres to find a phone. No one knew he was there. He had not told anyone where he would be. For three days and two nights it had poured unrelentingly, and the icy rain had swamped the tobacco in his pipe. Perhaps all told, three farm labourers in clogs had walked past. They had stared at him suspiciously and hurried on their way. Maigret had had nothing to eat with him, nothing to drink and, worst of all, by the end of day two, he ran out of matches for his pipe.

Lucas had another under his belt, as part of what was called The Case of the Halfwit Invalid. To keep watch on a small hotel – to be specific, it was on the corner of Rue de Birague, just off Places des Vosges – he had been installed in a room on the other side of the street, disguised as a paralysed old relic. Every morning a nurse sat him down by the window, where he stayed all day. He wore a fan-shaped false beard. He was fed with a spoon. That had lasted for ten days, and afterwards he could hardly use his legs.

Maigret now recalled these and a few other such tales and sensed that the stake-out he was beginning would become no less famous. At any rate, one to be savoured – especially by him.

It was almost a game, but he was playing it with total seriousness. At about seven o'clock, for example, just as Lucas was about to leave, he had asked him quite casually:

'Care for a little glass of something?'

The shutters of the bar were closed, as they had been when he had got there. The lights were on. The atmosphere inside was like that of any small bar after hours, with the tables set out and sawdust scattered on the floor.

Maigret went to get the drinks from the shelves behind the counter.

'Picon-grenadine? Export-cassis?'

'An export.'

And as if he were trying to identify with the dead barowner, Maigret had served himself a Suze.

'Who do you reckon could to do the job?'

'There's Chevrier. His parents used to run a hotel at Moret-sur-Loing, and he helped them until he was called up for his military service.'

'Have a word with him this evening so he can make

arrangements. Cheers! He'll have to find a woman who can cook.'

'He'll manage.'

'Another?'

'No thanks. I'd better be off.'

'Send Moers to me here at once. Tell him to bring his bag of tricks.'

Maigret walked him to the door, glanced out briefly at the now deserted riverbank, the barrels lined up in rows and the barges moored for the night.

It was a small bar no different from many others you find not in Paris itself but in the suburbs, the typical small café which features in postcards or cheap prints. The house stood on a corner. It had one storey, a red-tile roof and yellow walls on which was traced in large brown letters: 'Au Petit Albert'. And on each side, with amateurish flourishes: 'Wines – All Day Snacks'.

In the yard at the back, under an awning, Maigret had found half barrels painted green and containing shrubs which in summer would be put outside on the pavement with two or three tables to make a terrace.

He had now made himself at home in the empty building. Since no fires had been lit for several days, the air was cold and damp. Several times he had cast dubious glances at the large stove in the middle of the bar, which had a chimney pipe that rose black and gleaming into the air before disappearing through a wall.

Why not after all, since there was an almost full bucket of coal?

Under the same awning at the back he found kindling

next to a small axe and a chopping block. There were some old newspapers in one corner of the kitchen.

A few minutes later the fire was roaring in the stove, and the inspector was standing in front of it with his feet firmly planted and his hands behind his back, in that characteristic pose.

Basically, Lucas' old woman was not as crazy as all that. They had gone to her house. In the taxi on the way, she had talked volubly all the time, but now and then she glanced at them slyly to gauge the effect she was producing.

Her house was less than a hundred metres away. It was small, just two storeys, what they call a detached house with a small garden. Maigret had wondered how, given the unalterable fact that her house was on the same side of the street, she had been able to see what was going on some considerable distance along her pavement, especially after night had fallen.

'You didn't stay out on the pavement all that time?'

'No.'

'Nor on your doorstep?'

'I was in my house.'

She was right. The front room, which was amazingly neat and clean, had not only windows that gave on to the street but a side window which faced towards the Petit Albert and thus offered a view of a large part of the street. Since there were no shutters, it was only natural that the headlights of a parked car should have attracted the attention of the old lady.

'Were you alone here at the time?'

'Madame Chauffier was with me.'

A midwife who lived in a street a little further along. She had been checked out. It was true. Contrary to what might have been expected by anyone who had seen the old woman, the inside of the house had the same domestic look as the houses of all spinsters. There was none of the clutter with which fortune-tellers normally surround themselves. On the contrary, the plain deal furniture came straight from Boulevard Barbès, and there was light-brown linoleum on the floor,

'It was bound to happen,' she said. 'Have you seen what's written above the front of his café? Either he's one of them or else it's sacrilege.'

She had put water for the coffee on to boil. She was absolutely determined to make Maigret drink a cup. She explained to him that the Petit Albert was a book of magic dating from the fourteenth or fifteenth century.

'But what if his name happens to be Albert? And if he is really little?' replied Maigret.

'As a matter of fact he is short, I know. I've seen him many times. But that's not a proper reason. There are matters with which it is unwise to meddle.'

About Albert's wife, she said:

'Tall woman, dark hair, not very clean. I wouldn't like to eat anything she cooked. It always reeks of garlic.'

'How long have the shutters been closed?'

'I don't know. The day after the day I saw the car I stayed in bed. I had flu. When I was up and about again, the café was shut. I thought: and good riddance too.'

'Was it a noisy place?'

'No. Hardly anyone ever went there. But those men

working the crane you can see on the wharf used to go there for their lunch. There was also the cellarman from Cess the wine merchants. And men from the boats would go there and have a drink at the counter.'

She had asked particularly about which newspapers her photo would be in.

'But I must insist that they don't say in print that I tell fortunes. It would be a bit like them saying that you're just a policeman on the beat.'

'I wouldn't take offence.'

'It wouldn't be good for me, professionally.'

Time to get moving! He was done with the old woman. He had drunk his coffee and then Lucas and he had walked to the café on the corner. It was Lucas who had automatically tried the lever handle of the door. It was open.

That was odd. A small bar whose door had been left unlocked for four days and had survived unscathed, with bottles on the shelves behind the bar and cash in the till.

The bottom of the walls was painted in shiny brown gloss up to a metre from floor level, then pale-green above it. There were the same advertising calendars as are found in every country café.

Basically, the Petit Albert was not really as Parisian as all that, or rather, like most Parisians, it had stuck to its country roots. Just by looking at it, it was obvious it had been done out like this deliberately, with almost loving care, and its like would have been found in any village in France.

The same was true of the bedroom upstairs: Maigret, with his hands in his pockets, had inspected the premises from top to bottom. Lucas had followed him with some amusement because, with his overcoat and hat removed, Maigret seemed to be actually taking possession of a new house. In less than half an hour, he had made himself more or less at home and from time to time went and stood behind the bar.

'Well, one thing's for sure: Nine isn't here.'

He had looked everywhere for some trace of her from cellar to attic and also searched the yard and the small garden, which was cluttered with old chests and empty bottles.

'What do you think, Lucas?'

'I don't know, sir.'

In the bar there were just eight tables, four arranged along one wall, with two facing them and the last two in the middle of the room, by the stove. It was to one of the latter that the two men kept being drawn from time to time, because the sawdust under the legs of one of the chairs had been carefully swept up.

Why, if not to remove bloodstains?

But who had cleared away the victim's plates and cutlery? Who had washed them and the wine glasses?

'Maybe they came back later?' suggested Lucas.

But there was one very curious thing. Whereas everything in the whole place was neat and tidy, a bottle, just the one, had been opened and left on the counter. Maigret had been careful not to touch it. It was a bottle of cognac, and it could only be supposed that whoever had helped himself – or themselves – had not bothered with glasses but had drunk straight from the bottle.

The unknown visitors had been upstairs. They had

rummaged through all the drawers but had stuffed under-wear and other contents back inside them before shutting them again.

The oddest thing of all was that two frames hanging on the bedroom wall, which had probably contained photo-graphs, were now empty.

It was not Albert's appearance that they had wanted to suppress: there was another picture of him standing on the chest of drawers: cheerful, round face, kiss-curl over his forehead, the look of a comedian about him, just as the owner of the Caves du Beaujolais had said.

A taxi pulled up outside. The sound of footsteps on the pavement. Maigret walked to the door and drew back the bolt.

'Come in,' he said to Moers, who was carrying a rather heavy case. 'Have you eaten? No? Would you like an aperitif?'

It turned out to be one of the most curious evenings and strangest nights of his life. From time to time he would go and watch Moers, who had set to work on a lengthy task, looking everywhere, first in the bar itself, then the kitchen, the bedroom, in all the rooms in the building, for the faintest trace of fingerprints.

'Whoever picked up this bottle first,' he said, 'was wear-ing rubber gloves.'

He had also taken samples of sawdust from near the all-important table. Meanwhile, Maigret had searched a dustbin and found remnants of cod.

Only a few hours earlier his dead man had no name and in Maigret's mind he had been just a blurred figure. Now not only did they have a photo of him, but he was living in his house, using his tables and chairs, fingering the clothes which had belonged to him and handling objects which had been his. Almost the moment they had arrived it was with a certain satisfaction that he had pointed out to Lucas a coat on a clothes hanger upstairs: it was a jacket made of the same material as the dead man's trousers.

In other words, he had been right. Albert had come home and changed his clothes, as was his habit.

'Do you think, Moers, old son, that it's very long since anyone was here?'

'I'd say someone was here today,' replied the young man, after examining the traces of alcohol on the counter next to the open bottle.

It was quite possible. The place had been left wide open to all and sundry. But pedestrians passing by didn't know. When people see closed shutters, it rarely occurs to them to try the handle of the door to see if it is locked.

'So they were looking for something, right?'

'That's my view too.'

Something not too big, most likely some sort of paper, because they had even opened a very small cardboard box which had contained a pair of earrings.

Odd was the word for the dinner which Maigret and Moers had eaten together in the bar of the café. Maigret had taken charge of serving it up. In the pantry he had found sausage, tins of sardines and some Dutch cheese. He had gone down to the cellar and tapped a barrel, which gave a muddy, bluish wine. There were also full bottles of wine, but he had not touched them.

'Are you going to stay here, chief?'

'Certainly. I don't suppose anyone will show up tonight, but I don't feel like going home.'

'Do you want me to keep you company?'

'Thanks, old son, but no. I'd much rather you went straight off and started on your analyses.'

Moers missed nothing, not even the woman's hair caught in a large-toothed comb on the dressing table upstairs. Very few sounds drifted in from outside. Passersby were rare. From time to time, especially after midnight, there was the roar of a lorry coming in from the outskirts on its way to Les Halles.

Maigret had phoned his wife.

'Are you sure you're not going to catch another cold?'

'Don't worry. I've lit the stove. In a while I'll make myself a grog.'

'Won't you get any sleep tonight?'

'Of course I will. I have a choice between a bed and a couch.'

'Are the sheets clean?'

'There are clean ones in a cupboard on the landing.'

In fact, it meant remaking the bed with cold sheets and sleeping in them. He thought about it and opted for the couch.

Moers left around one in the morning. Maigret refilled the stove to the top, made himself a stiff grog, checked that everything was in order and, after bolting the door, climbed up the spiral staircase on leaden legs like a man on his way to bed.

There was a dressing gown in the wardrobe, blue, made

of soft flannel with artificial silk lapels. But it was far too small and not broad enough for him. The slippers at the foot of the bed weren't his size either.

He kept his socks on, wrapped himself in a blanket and settled on the couch with a pillow under his head. The upstairs windows did not have shutters. The light from a gas streetlamp came through the elaborately patterned curtains and cast baroque shapes on the walls.

He looked at them through half-closed eyes as he puffed gently on one last pipe. He was acclimatizing himself. He was trying the house for size, just as he might have tried a new coat. The smell of the place was already becoming familiar. It was sweet and tart at the same time and it reminded him of the country.

Why had the photos of Nine been removed? Why had she disappeared, deserting her home, without even taking the money in the till? True, it amounted to less than a hundred francs. Obviously Albert kept his money somewhere else, and that was what the intruders had taken just as they had taken all his private papers.

The oddest thing was that a thorough search of the whole building had been made without disturbing anything or producing any mess whatsoever. The clothes in the wardrobe had been checked through but had not been removed from their hangers. Photos had been torn from their frames but the frames had been put back on their nails.

Maigret fell asleep and when he heard someone knocking on the shutters downstairs he would have sworn that he had dropped off only a few minutes before.

But it was seven o'clock and light. The sun was shining on the Seine, where the barges were beginning to move and tugs were sounding their hooters.

He took a moment to slip his shoes on without doing up the laces and went down the stairs, hair uncombed, collar unbuttoned and his jacket creased.

It was Chevrier and a rather good-looking woman wearing a blue two-piece suit and a small red hat on her frizzed hair.

'Here we are, sir.'

Chevrier had been with the Police Judiciaire for only three or four years. He did not look like a goat, as his name suggested, but more like a sheep; the contours of his face and body were soft and round. The woman tugged him by the sleeve. He understood and stammered:

'Sorry! Detective chief inspector, may I introduce my wife?'

'No need to worry,' she said pluckily. 'I've done this before. My mother used to run the inn in our village and sometimes, with just a couple of serving girls to help us, we'd lay on wedding receptions for fifty or more people.'

She walked straight to the percolator and asked her husband: 'Pass me your matches.'

The gas went 'pft', and a few minutes later a smell of coffee spread through the house.

Chevrier had taken good care to wear black trousers and a white shirt. He too was dressed for the part. He took his place behind the counter and moved a few things round.

'Shall we open?'

'Yes. It must be time.'

'Which of us will get the groceries?' asked the wife.

'In a while I want you to take a taxi and buy what you need from wherever is closest.'

'Will fricandeau of veal with sorrel be all right?'

She had brought a white apron with her. She was very cheerful, very vivacious. It was as if they were preparing for a day trip, or playing a game.

'We can take the shutters down now,' said Maigret. 'If customers ask questions, say you are just standing in.'

He went back upstairs, found a razor, shaving soap and a brush. After all, why not? Albert appeared to have been a man of clean habits and fit. So, taking his time, he washed and shaved. When he came downstairs, Chevrier's wife had already gone shopping. Two men were leaning on the counter, two barge men, drinking coffee with calvados. They didn't care who owned the bar. They were probably just passing through. They were talking about a lock which had almost had one sluice stove in by a tug the night before.

'What can I get you, sir?'

Maigret preferred to help himself. It was actually the first time in his life that he had poured himself a glass of rum from the bottle behind the counter of a bar. Suddenly, he laughed.

'Just thinking about Monsieur Coméliau,' he explained.

He tried to imagine the examining magistrate walking into the Petit Albert and finding the detective chief inspector standing behind the counter, with one of his officers.

But if anything was to be learned, there was no other way. Wouldn't the men who had murdered the bar's owner be surprised to find the place open as usual?

87

And what about Nine, if she were still alive?

At about nine o'clock, the ancient clairvoyant walked past then walked back again, even pressing her nose to the window before moving off, muttering to herself, carrying a net bag full of shopping in one hand.

Madame Maigret had just phoned to find out how her husband was.

'Can I bring you anything? Your toothbrush, for example?'

'No thanks. I've asked someone to buy me one.'

'Monsieur Coméliau phoned.'

'I hope you didn't give him this number.'

'No. I just told him you went out yesterday evening and hadn't come back yet.'

Chevrier's wife got out of a taxi, from which she took wooden boxes full of vegetables and provisions wrapped in paper. When Maigret called her 'madame', she said:

'Oh, just call me Irma. You'll see, it's what the customers will all call me from the word go. That's fine with you, Émile, that he can . . . ?'

But hardly any customers came. Three bricklayers who were working on scaffolding in a street nearby came in for their break. They brought bread and sausage with them and ordered two litres of red wine.

'It's a good job this place has reopened! Before, it was a ten-minute walk from here before we found somewhere to get a drink!'

They weren't puzzled to see new faces.

'The previous owner has retired, then?'

One of them commented:

'He was a decent sort.'

'Had you known him long?'

'Just for the couple of weeks we've been working on a site round the corner. We move around a lot, you see.'

But Maigret, whom they saw prowling in the background, made them curious.

'Who's that, then? He looks like he lives here.'

Without missing a breath, Chevrier replied:

'Sh! That's my father-in-law.'

Various pans were simmering on the kitchen stove. The whole place was coming to life. A vinegary sun flooded in through the front windows of the bar. Chevrier, with his sleeves rolled up and held by elastic, had swept up the sawdust.

The telephone rang.

'It's for you, sir. Moers.'

Poor Moers had not slept all night. He hadn't had much success with the fingerprints. Prints there were, of all kinds, on the bottles and furniture. For the most part they were already old and overlapped each other. The clearest, which he had forwarded to the anthropometrics lab, could not be matched with any set on file.

'They searched the whole place wearing rubber gloves. Only one thing gave any result at all: the sawdust. Analysis showed up traces of blood.'

'Human blood?'

'I'll know that in an hour. But I'm virtually certain . . .'

Lucas, who that morning had had his own share of the

work to do, arrived about eleven o'clock, looking bright and breezy. Maigret noticed that he had chosen to wear a light-coloured tie.

'An export-cassis,' he called to his colleague, Chevrier, with a wink.

Irma had hung a slate by the door on which, under the words 'Today's Special', she had chalked: 'fricandeau of veal with sorrel'. She could be heard rushing around and on that day she would not have changed places with any-one for anything in the world.

'Let's go upstairs,' Maigret said to Lucas.

They went up to the bedroom and stood by the win-dow, which had been opened because the weather was so mild. The crane was working by the water's edge, lifting barrels out of the entrails of a barge. Whistles sounded, chains clanked and on the shimmering surface of the water there was the constant bustle of panting, fussing tugs.

'His name is Albert Rochain. I went to the Central Reg-istry. He was issued with a licence four years ago.'

'Did you manage to get the name of his wife?'

'No, the licence was in his sole name. I went to the town hall, where they were unable to give me any information. If he had a wife, he was already married when he moved into the area.'

'You tried the local police?'

'Nothing there. It appears that there was never any trouble in these premises. The police were never called here.'

Maigret's eye remained fixed on the photo of his dead

man on the chest of drawers, which showed him still smiling.

'Chevrier will probably find out more later from the customers.'

'Are you staying here?'

'We could have lunch downstairs like a pair of casual customers. Any news from Torrence and Janvier?'

'They're still out questioning race-goers.'

'If you can reach them by phone, tell them to concentrate on Vincennes.'

Always the same old refrain: the track at Vincennes was what might be called the 'local' race-course. And Albert, like Maigret, was a creature of habit.

'Aren't people surprised to see that the café has reopened?'

'Not particularly. Some of the neighbours have turned up on the pavement for a look. They probably think that Albert has sold up.'

At noon, they were both sitting at a table by the window, and Irma served them herself. A few customers were seated at other tables, notably crane drivers.

'So Albert finally hit the jackpot, then?' one of them called out to Chevrier.

'He's had to go out of town for a while.'

'And you've replaced him? Did he take Nine with him? Maybe now we'll get something to eat with a bit less garlic in it, which wouldn't be a bad thing! Not that there's anything wrong with garlic, except it gets on the breath . . .'

The man pinched Irma's behind as she passed. Chevrier

did not react and even bore Lucas' amused glance in silence.

'A good sort, right enough! Too bad he was so mad about the races! . . . But listen, if he had someone to cover for him, how come he closed the café for four days? Especially without letting his customers know? The first day we had to traipse all the way to Charenton bridge to get a bite to eat. No thanks, dearie, I never eat camembert. I have a small cream cheese, just one, every day. And Jules has Roquefort . . .'

Even so, they were intrigued and spoke in whispers. Irma in particular was a subject of some interest.

'Chevrier won't be able to stand this for too long,' murmured Lucas into Maigret's ear. 'He's only been married for two years. If these morons keep letting their hands stray all over his wife's backside, they'll soon feel the weight of his fists on their chins.'

It wasn't that bad. But as he brought the men their drinks, Chevrier said firmly:

'That's my wife.'

'Congratulations . . . But not to worry! We're not particular!'

And they roared with laughter. They weren't nasty characters but they sensed vaguely that Albert's stand-in was riled.

'Albert, now, he made good and sure . . . There was no danger anyone would steal Nine off him . . .'

'Why not?'

'Don't you know her?'

'Never set eyes on her.'

'You haven't missed anything, chum. She would have been safe in a roomful of Senegalese. Lovely girl, of course . . . That's right, Jules, isn't it?'

'How old is she?'

'I don't know as how you could put any age on her. What do you reckon, Jules?'

'I dunno. She's ageless. Maybe thirty? Or perhaps fifty? It depends which side you look at her from. If it's the side with the good eye, she's not too bad. But if it's the other one . . .'

'She has a squint?'

'And how! The man he asks if she's got a squint! I tell you, she could look at the toes of your shoes and the top of the Eiffel Tower without moving her head!'

'Does Albert love her?'

'Albert is a man who likes the easy life, if you take my meaning. Look, your missus makes a good, I'd even say excellent, stew. But I bet you're the one who gets up at six and trots off to Les Halles to buy whatever she needs. Maybe you even give her a hand peeling the spuds. But an hour after, it's not her who's doing all the washing up while you swan off to the races . . .'

'But that's how it works with Nine! Albert lives the life of Riley! Not to mention that she must have had money of her own.'

Why at this point did Lucas take a sideways look at Maigret? Wasn't it rather as if the inspector's dead man had just been dragged through the dirt?

The crane driver went on:

'I dunno how she earned it, but with her looks it couldn't have been by going on the game . . .'

Maigret did not flinch. There was even a faint smile playing about his lips. He was not missing one word of what was being said, and those words automatically conjured up images. The picture of Albert was being completed piece by piece, and in the process Maigret appeared to lose none of his affection for the man who was now clearly emerging.

'What part of the country are you two from, then?'

'I'm from the Berry,' answered Irma.

'Me, I'm from the Cher,' said Chevrier.

'So it wasn't in your home towns that you met Albert. He's from the north, or rather north-east . . . Isn't he from Tourcoing, Jules?'

'Roubaix.'

'Same thing.'

Maigret broke into the conversation, which did not seem the least surprising in a bar frequented by regulars.

'Didn't he used to work somewhere around Gare du Nord?'

'Yes, in the Cadran. He was a waiter in the same brasserie for ten or twelve years before setting up on his own here.'

It was no accident that Maigret had asked the question. He knew that when northerners move to Paris, they seem to find it very hard to settle far from their station. They form a colony more or less, centred around Rue de Maubeuge.

'It couldn't have been there that he met Nine.'

'Whether it was there or somewhere else, he certainly hit the jackpot. It wasn't on account of his winnings, of course. It was on account of never having to worry about money ever again.'

'Was she from the Midi?'

'And then some!'

'You mean Marseilles?'

'Toulouse! She had an accent you could cut with a knife! Next to her, that announcer on Radio-Toulouse has just got a bit of a twang . . . Right, let's have the bill . . . By the way, landlord, aren't we forgetting our manners?'

Chevrier frowned, disconcerted. But Maigret understood and it was he who replied:

'He's right! When a bar gets a new landlord, it's drinks on the house!'

There were only seven customers all that lunchtime. One of them was a cellarman from Cess, middle-aged and with a surly manner, who ate by himself in a corner and found fault with everything: with the cooking, which wasn't the same, with his table, which wasn't his usual table, with the white wine he was given instead of the red he was used to . . .

'This place is going to turn into a dump just like all the others,' he grumbled as he left. 'It's always the same.'

Chevrier was no longer enjoying himself as much as he had that morning. Only Irma seemed to stay cheerful, juggling with the dishes and the piles of plates, and she attacked the washing-up, humming a tune to herself.

At 1.30, only Maigret and Lucas were still in the bar. There followed the quiet, slow period when they saw a customer only from time to time, a passer-by who happened to be thirsty, or a couple of river men who were passing the time while their boats were being loaded.

Maigret smoked his pipe quietly, paunch very much in

evidence, for he had eaten a great deal, perhaps to please Irma. The sun warmed one of his ears, and he wore an expression of utter contentment. Then all of a sudden the sole of one shoe came down heavily on Lucas' toes.

A man had just walked past on the pavement. He had stared intently into the bar, paused uncertainly, then turned and was now approaching the door.

He was of average height. He was not wearing a hat or a cap. He had red hair, and there were reddish blotches on his face. His eyes were blue and his lips fleshy.

He reached for the lever handle. He entered, still hesitating. There was something loose-limbed about his bearing and an odd reticence in his gestures.

His shoes were worn and had not been polished for several days. His dark suit was shiny, his shirt of dubious cleanliness and his tie badly knotted.

He was like a cat stepping warily into an unfamiliar room, observing everything around it and alert to possible danger. He must have been of less than average intelligence – village idiots often have eyes like his, which expressed only low cunning and mistrust.

Was it that Maigret and Lucas had aroused his curiosity? He was suspicious of them, sidled up to the bar without taking his eyes off them and tapped the metal counter with a coin.

Chevrier emerged from the kitchen, where he was eating his lunch in a corner.

'What'll it be?'

The man hesitated again. He appeared to have a bad cold. He growled something incomprehensible then gave up trying to speak and instead pointed at the bottle of cognac on a shelf.

It was straight into Chevrier's eyes that he now looked. There was something here that he did not understand, something beyond his comprehension.

With the toe of one shoe, Maigret unobtrusively nudged Lucas' foot again.

The whole episode was brief, though it seemed long. The man dug in his pockets for change with his left hand while with the right he raised the glass to his lips and downed the contents in one gulp.

The strong spirit made him cough. His eyes watered.

He tossed some coins on the counter and, with a few very long, quick strides, was gone. Through the window, they could see him scurry off in the direction of Quai de Bercy, pause and turn round.

'Over to you,' said Maigret to Lucas. 'But I'm afraid he'll lose you . . .'

Lucas hurried out.

'Phone for a taxi!' Maigret called to Chevrier, 'and quick about it!'

Quai de Bercy was long and straight, without sidestreets. Maybe in a car he would be in time to catch up with the man before he gave Lucas the slip.

5.

As the pace of the pursuit grew faster, Maigret had a growing feeling that he had done it all before. It was something that occasionally happened to him in dreams, the kind of dreams which even when he was a boy he had feared most. He would be proceeding through some generally ambiguous surroundings and suddenly feel that he had been there before, that he had already done the same things and spoken the same words. It made his head spin, especially when he was aware that he was actually living through situations he had already lived through once before.

He had already followed the course of this manhunt, which now began on Quai de Charenton, from his office when Albert's panicky voice had kept him abreast hour by hour of the progress of his growing fear. And now the tension was mounting again. Along the whole length of Quai de Bercy, now almost deserted, the man who was walking past the row of wrought-iron gates with long, springy strides would turn round from time to time and then accelerate away when he invariably saw the stocky figure of Lucas.

Maigret, sitting next to the driver of his taxi, followed at a distance and was struck by the difference between the two men! There was something animal-like about the first man's walk and the way he kept looking over his shoulder.

Even when he started to run, his movements remained graceful.

Hot on his heels, Lucas, flabby, his paunch sticking out a little as usual, made him think of those mongrel dogs which look like sausages with legs but stay with the scent of the boar better than the most renowned breeds of bloodhounds.

You would have backed the redhead over him every time. Maigret too: when he saw that the man was making the most of the fact that there was no one about on the Quai to forge ahead, he told the driver to go faster. But there was no need. The odd thing was that Lucas did not look as if he was running. He retained his conventional air of a respectable Parisian out for a stroll and just went waddling on.

When the stranger heard the sound of footsteps behind him, when he half-turned his head and saw Maigret in a taxi drawing almost level with him, he realized that there was nothing to be gained from getting out of breath and attracting attention to himself and slowed to a more normal pace.

During the course of that afternoon, thousands of people would pass them in the streets and public squares and, as had been the case with Albert, not one of them would have any inkling of the drama which was being played out.

By the time they were crossing Pont d'Austerlitz, the foreigner – in Maigret's mind, he was definitely a foreigner – was beginning to look more anxious. He continued along Quai Henri-IV. He was getting ready to make his move, that much was clear from his manner. Then, just as they reached the Saint-Paul district, with the taxi still following him, he took off again, this time darting into the maze of narrow streets which stretches between Rue Saint-Antoine and the embankment.

Maigret almost lost him when a lorry blocked one of the alleyways.

Children playing on the pavement watched the two men run past. Maigret eventually caught up with them two streets further on. Lucas had barely raised a sweat and still looked very respectable in his buttoned-up overcoat. He even had the presence of mind to wink at Maigret as if to say:

'Not to worry!'

He was not to know that the hunt, followed by Maigret from the front seat of a car without tiring himself out, would last for several hours. Nor that it would turn more relentless the longer it went on.

It was after the phone call that the man began to lose his confidence. He had walked into a small bar in Rue Saint-Antoine. Lucas had followed him in.

'Is he going to arrest him?' asked the taxi-driver, who knew Maigret.

'No.'

'Why not?'

To his mind, a man who is being followed is a man who will be arrested sooner or later. What was the point of pursuing him like this, of inflicting such pointless cruelty? He was reacting the way the uninitiated do when a hunt passes by.

Paying no attention to Lucas, the stranger had asked for a phone token and shut himself away in the booth. Through the windows of the café, Lucas could be seen making the most of the enforced halt to sink a large glass of beer. The sight made Maigret feel thirsty.

The phone call was a long one: almost five minutes. Two or three times, Lucas became concerned. He went to the door of the phone booth and looked through the spy-hole to make sure that nothing had happened to his man.

Afterwards, they stood side by side at the counter, without speaking, as if they had never seen each other before. The man's expression had changed. He looked around him apprehensively and seemed to be watching for the right moment, though he had probably realized that there would be no more right moments for him.

After some time, he paid and left. He headed off towards Place de la Bastille, completed almost a full circuit of the square, walked briefly along Boulevard Richard-Lenoir, just a few minutes from Maigret's apartment, but turned right along Rue de la Roquette. It was not long before he was lost. It was patently obvious that he did not know the area. Two or three more times he had thoughts about making a run for it. But there were too many people about or perhaps he would catch sight of a policeman's peaked képi at the next junction.

At this point, he began to drink. He went into bars, not to phone, but to gulp down a glass of cheap cognac. Lucas had decided not to follow him inside any more.

In one of these bars, a man spoke to him. He stared at

him without answering, like a man who has been addressed in a language he doesn't understand.

Maigret could now see why from the very start, from the moment the man had walked into the Petit Albert, he had sensed that there was something foreign about him. It wasn't so much that the cut of his clothes or his cast of features was not French. It was rather the cautious behaviour of someone who is not at home in his surroundings, who does not understand and cannot make himself understood.

There was sunshine in the streets. It was very mild. Concierges in the Picpus district, like concierges in small provincial towns, had put a chair outside their front door.

What a merry dance they were led before they reached Boulevard Voltaire and finally Place de la République, where the man finally regained his bearings!

He went down the steps into the Métro. Was he still hoping to shake Lucas off? If he did, he must have realized that his stratagem would not work, for Maigret saw the pair coming back up through the exit.

Rue Réaumur . . . Another detour . . . Rue de Turbigo . . . Then along Rue Chapon to Rue Beaubourg.

'This is his patch,' thought Maigret.

It was palpable. Just from the way the stranger looked about him, it was obvious he recognized every shop. He was at home. Perhaps he lived in one of the many run-down hotels?

He kept hesitating, stopping at street corners. Something was preventing him doing what he wanted to do. In this way he progressed as far as Rue de Rivoli, which marked the limit of that area of impoverished streets.

He did not cross it. Going along Rue des Archives, he went back into the ghetto and was soon walking along Rue des Rosiers.

'He doesn't want us to know where he lives!'

But why not? And whom had he phoned? Had he asked one of his cronies for help? What could he expect from that quarter?

'I'm really sorry for the poor devil,' breathed the taxi-driver. 'Are you sure he's a crook?'

No! Not even a petty crook! But there was no choice but to follow him. It was his only chance of getting a new lead on Albert's murder.

The man was sweating profusely. His nose was running. From time to time he would take a large green handker-chief from his pocket. And he was continuing to drink steadily, moving away from a central core formed by Rue du Roi-de-Sicile, Rue des Étouffes and Rue de la Verrerie, a hub around which he went on circling without ever venturing inside it.

He would move away and then, irresistibly drawn to it, would come back again. He slowed, became more uncertain. He would turn to face Lucas. Then he looked around for the taxi and glared at it. Who knows? If the cab had not been following him so closely, perhaps he would have tried to get Lucas off his back by luring him into an alley and dealing with him.

When it started to get dark, the streets began to bustle with activity. Sauntering crowds filled the pavements and streets lined with low, gloomy houses. As soon as the first signs of spring appear, the inhabitants of this part of Paris begin to live outside. The doors of shops and the windows of houses were open. The reek of dirt and poverty caught in the throat, and sometimes a woman would throw her slops out into the road.

Lucas must have been at the end of his tether, though he did not show it. Maigret thought that he should take the first opportunity to have him relieved. He felt rather ashamed of tagging along in a taxi, the way visitors follow a fox-hunt in cars.

There were junctions which they had crossed four or five times. Suddenly, the man hit on a new tactic. He slipped into the gloomy passage of a house. Lucas stopped at the door. Maigret signalled him to follow.

'Be careful!' he called from his seat in the car.

A few moments later, both men emerged. It was obvious that the stranger had gone into the first house he had come to, hoping he could lose his police tail.

He repeated the same manoeuvre. The second time, Lucas found him sitting at the top of the stairs.

Shortly before six, they were back on the corner of Rue du Roi-de-Sicile and Rue Vieille-du-Temple, in what looked and felt like a thieves' kitchen. The stranger paused again. Then he darted out into the street, which was filled with poor people. Lights in frosted-glass globes hung outside several of the hotels. The shops were narrow-fronted, and alleyways led to mysterious courtyards.

He did not get far. He had covered about six metres and then a shot rang out, a dry sound, no louder than a tyre bursting. The activity in the street took a few moments to subside, as if slowed in its reactions by its collective momentum. The taxi had stopped of its own accord, as if in amazement.

Then there was the sound of running footsteps. Lucas leaped forward. There was a second shot.

The swirling crowds made it impossible to see anything. Maigret did not know if the inspector had been hit. He had got out of the cab and was rushing towards the wounded foreigner.

He was on the pavement, sitting up. He wasn't dead. He was supporting himself on one hand and holding his chest with the other. He raised his head and looked up reproachfully at Maigret.

Then a shadow fell across those blue eyes. A woman said:

'It's a crying shame!'

The man's torso swayed and fell at an angle across the pavement.

He was dead.

Lucas returned empty-handed but unharmed. The second shot had missed him. The assailant had tried to fire a third time, but his gun must have jammed. Lucas had not got much of a look at him.

'I wouldn't be able to recognize him,' he said. 'But I think he had dark hair.'

Without seeming to, the crowd had helped the murderer to escape by, as it were, accidentally getting in the way. At no time had Lucas found his path unimpeded.

And now people surrounded them, hostile, even threatening. In those mean streets it did not take them long to sniff out plain-clothed policemen.

But a uniformed officer arrived and pushed the gawping crowd back.

'Get an ambulance,' Maigret growled to him, 'but first use your whistle and get two or three of your colleagues here.'

Leaving nothing to chance, he murmured orders to Lucas, whom he left at the scene with the officers. He took another look at the dead man. He would have liked to search his pockets at once, but he felt oddly reluctant at the thought of doing it in full view of all those curious bystanders. It would be too pointed, too professional an action and would be construed here as desecration or even as a provocation.

'Be careful,' he told Lucas in a bare whisper. 'There are bound to be more of them around . . .'

He was only a stone's throw from Quai des Orfèvres, and the taxi dropped him there. He climbed straight up to the commissioner's office and knocked, without first waiting to be announced.

'Another murder,' he said. 'This one was shot right under our noses, like a rabbit, in the middle of a street.'

'Do you have a name?'

'Lucas will be here in a few minutes, as soon as the body has been taken away. Can you let me have twenty or so men? There's an entire neighbourhood which I want to close off.'

'Which neighbourhood?'

'Roi-de-Sicile.'

It was the turn of the commissioner of the Police Judiciaire to scowl. Maigret went straight to the office where the inspectors were based, picked out several and gave them their orders.

Then he went off to find the detective chief inspector who headed up the Vice Squad.

'Could you let me have on temporary secondment an inspector who knows Rue du Roi-de-Sicile, Rue des Rosiers and the streets round about like the back of his hand? There must be a fair number of girls on the game thereabouts.'

'Too many.'

'In half an hour or so, he'll be given a photo.'

'Another stiff?'

'Unfortunately, yes. But this time his face wasn't rearranged for him.'

'I see.'

'There must be several of them hiding up around there. Take care. They're killers.'

Next he went down to the Hotel Agency. He asked for more or less the same favour.

Speed was of the essence. He checked to make sure that the inspectors had left to begin patrolling in and around the neighbourhood. Then he phoned forensics.

'Have you got those photos?'

'You can send someone round for them in a few minutes. The body has arrived. We're working on it.'

He had a feeling that there was something he was forgetting. He remained where he was, ready to be off, scratching his head, and suddenly the face of Coméliau, the examining magistrate, sprang in to his mind.

And a good job it did!

'Hello! Good evening, sir. It's Maigret.'

'Ah, Detective Chief Inspector! And how are you getting on with the man you reckoned ran a small bar?'

'Actually he did run a small café, sir.'

'Have you identified him?'

'Identified him one hundred per cent.'

'Are you making progress with your investigation?'

'We've already managed to come up with a second corpse.'

He pictured the examining magistrate suddenly straightening up at the other end of the line.

'What did you say?'

'We've got another body. But this time, it's a member of the opposing group.'

'You mean it was the police who killed him?'

'No. This other lot took care of it themselves.'

'What "other lot" are you talking about?'

'His cronies, probably.'

'Have they been arrested?'

'Not yet.'

He lowered his voice.

'I'm afraid, sir, that it's going to be a long and difficult investigation. This is a very nasty business. They are killers, you know.'

'Am I to conclude that if they hadn't killed anybody there wouldn't have been a case to investigate?'

'You misunderstand me. They kill, in cold blood, to defend themselves. That's quite rare, you know, despite what the general public believes. They won't hesitate to gun down one of their own.'

'Why?'

'Probably because his cover was blown and might have led us to them. Also, it's a dangerous neighbourhood, one of the most dangerous in the whole of Paris. It's full of foreigners with no or false papers.'

'What are you proposing to do?'

'I'll follow procedure, because I have to, because I am personally accountable. We'll stage a raid tonight, but it won't come up with anything.'

'I hope at any rate that it won't result in further casualties.'

'I hope so too.'

'What time are you proposing to go ahead with it?'

'Usual time. About two in the morning.'

'I have a bridge party tonight. I'll make it last for as long as I can. Phone me as soon as the raid is over.'

'Very well, sir.'

'When will you let me have your report?'

'As soon as I have time to write it up. Probably not before tomorrow evening.'

'How's the bronchitis?'

'What bronchitis?'

He had forgotten all about it.

Lucas walked into his office, holding a red card in his hand. Maigret could see what it was. It was a trade union membership card made out in the name of Victor Poliensky, a Czech national, an unskilled worker in the Citroën factories.

'What's the address, Lucas?'

'132, Quai de Javel.'

'Wait a moment. The address is vaguely familiar. I think

it's probably that insalubrious rooming house on the corner of the Quai and a street whose name I've forgotten. We raided it about two years ago. Check and see if they have a telephone.'

The property was located further along the Seine, not far from the dark mass of the factory buildings, a run-down nest of furnished rooms full to overflowing with newly arrived foreigners who often slept three to a room despite police regulations. What was surprising was that the place was run by a woman and that she was quite capable of holding her own against all her tenants. She even cooked for them.

'Hello? Is that 132, Quai de Javel?'

A woman's husky voice.

'Is Poliensky there just now?'

She said nothing, taking her time before she answered.

'I mean Victor . . .'

'So? . . .'

'Is he there?'

'What's it to you?'

'I'm a friend of his.'

'You're a cop, that's what.'

'Let's suppose for argument's sake that this is the police. Does Poliensky still live at this address? I needn't add that anything you say will be checked.'

'I know how you operate.'

'Well?'

'He hasn't been here for more than six months.'

'Where did he work?'

'He worked for Citroën.'

'Has he been in France for long?'

'No idea.'

'Did he speak French?'

'No.'

'How long did he live under your roof?'

'About three months.'

'Did he have any friends? Did he get visitors?'

'No.'

'Were his papers in order?'

'Probably, because your hotel snoopers didn't mention anything to me.'

'Another question. Did he used to have his meals with you?'

'Usually.'

'Did he bother with women?'

'Listen, you dirty-minded swine, do you think I'm interested in that sort of thing?'

He hung up. Turning to Lucas, he said:

'Get on to Immigration.'

The Préfecture of Police had no record of the man in their files. This meant that the Czech was there illegally, like so many others, like the thousands who gravitate to the shadier parts of Paris. Most probably, like most of them, he had acquired a false identity card. There were many back-street operators in and around the Faubourg Saint-Antoine who supplied them for a set price.

'Find out from Citroën!'

The photos of the dead man had arrived and he distributed them to the inspectors from the Vice Squad and the Hotel Agency.

He went upstairs himself to Records to check progress on the fingerprinting.

There were no matches.

'Isn't Moers here?' he asked, putting his head round the laboratory door.

Moers ought not to have been there, because he had worked all night and through the day. But he didn't need much sleep. He had no family, no known girlfriend and no passion except his laboratory.

'Over here, chief!'

'I've got another corpse for you. But first, come to my office.'

They went down together. Lucas had spoken to the accounts department at Citroën.

'That old girl was right. He worked for them as an unskilled labourer for three months. He hasn't been on their books for six months.'

'Was he a good worker?'

'Not many absences. But they employ so many people that they don't know them individually. I asked if we came tomorrow and saw the foreman he worked under, would we get more information. It's no good. With skilled workers, yes. But the unskilled labourers, who are almost all foreigners, come and go, and no one gets to know them. There are always a few hundred of them waiting at the gates hoping to be taken on. They may work for three days, three weeks or three months and then they are never seen again. They get moved from site to site as and when they're needed.'

'Anything in his pockets?'

On his desk was a battered wallet. The leather must once have been green. In addition to the union membership card, it had contained a photo of a young woman. Round, fresh face with heavy plaits piled over the top of her head. Very probably Czech, a country girl.

'Two thousand-franc notes and three hundreds.'

'That's quite a lot,' said Maigret.

A long flick-knife with a narrow blade as sharp as a razor.

'Wouldn't you say, Moers, that this knife might well have been the one that killed Albert?'

'It's possible, chief.'

The handkerchief was greenish too. Victor Poliensky must have liked green.

'So you might think! It's not a cheerful thought, but you never know what your tests will show.'

A packet of Caporal cigarettes and a German-made lighter. Some small change. No keys.

'Are you sure, Lucas, that there weren't any keys?'

'Certain, sir.'

'Did they remove all his clothes?'

'Not yet. They're waiting for Moers.'

'Best be off, then! On this occasion, I don't have time to come with you. You're going to have to spend a part of tonight again working. You'll be dead beat.'

'I can easily manage two nights on the trot. It won't be the first time . . .'

Maigret asked to be put through to the Petit Albert.

'Anything new, Émile?'

'Nothing, sir. Much the same.'

'Had many customers?'

'Fewer than this morning. Some for an aperitif, but we've had hardly any takers for dinner.'

'Is your wife still enjoying playing landladies?'

'She's in her element. She's cleaned the bedroom from top to bottom, changed the sheets and we'll be snug up there. What about the man with red hair?'

'Dead.'

'What?'

'One of his low-life pals decided to put a bullet in his hide just because he thought he'd like to go home.'

He called in again at the inspectors' room. He couldn't afford to overlook anything.

'Anything come up on the yellow Citroën?'

'Nothing new. But there have been a few sightings of it around Barbès-Rochechouart.'

'Really! We've got to follow up on that lead.'

And again for geographical reasons. The Barbès district lies next to Gare du Nord, and Albert had worked for a long time as a waiter in a brasserie somewhere near the station.

'Hungry, Lucas?' asked Maigret.

'Not particularly. I can wait.'

'What about your wife?'

'I can phone home.'

'Right, I'll just phone home too and then I'll keep you with me.'

Even so, he was feeling rather tired and he didn't much feel like working by himself, especially since the night to come promised to be exhausting.

They both stopped off at the Brasserie Dauphine for an aperitif. It always came as a surprise when they were deep in an investigation to observe that life around them continued normally, that people still went about their lawful occasions and joked and laughed. What did it matter to them if a Czech had been shot on the pavement of Rue du Roi-de-Sicile? It was worth just a short paragraph in the papers.

Then one fine day they would learn that the murderer had been arrested. No one, save those directly involved, knew that a raid was being organized in the most densely populated and most combustible parts of Paris. Could they pick out the plainclothes police officers posted on the corner of every street, trying to look as inconspicuous as possible?

A few tarts, maybe, lurking in recesses from which they emerged from time to time to clutch at the arm of a possible customer, would flinch as they recognized the tell-tale figure of a member of the Vice Squad. They immediately assumed that they would be spending part of the night in the cells of the Préfecture. They were used to it. It happened to them at least once a month. Provided they were clean, they would be released at about ten o'clock the next morning.

Nor did the people who ran rented accommodation like it when officers came at unusual hours to check their registers. Of course, everything was all in order. Everything was always in order.

A photo would be thrust under their noses. They would make a show of looking at it very carefully, even making a point of going off to fetch their glasses.

'Do you know this man?'

'Never saw him before.'

'Do you have any Czechs staying here?'

'Some Polish, Italians, an Armenian, but no Czechs.'

'That's it.'

Routine. Further out, at Barbès, one of the inspectors whose job was making inquiries exclusively about the yellow car, was questioning garage owners, mechanics, officers on the beat, shopkeepers, concierges.

Routine.

Chevrier and his wife were playing at running a café down on Quai de Charenton and would shortly, after putting up the shutters, sit and chat by the large stove before going upstairs to settle into the bed that had belonged to Li'l Albert and wall-eyed Nine.

She was someone else who had to be traced. She was not known to the Vice Squad. What could have become of her? Did she know that her husband was dead? If she knew, why had she not come forward to identify his body after his picture had appeared in the papers? Other people had been unable to recognize him. But surely she . . . ?

Had the murderers abducted her? She hadn't been in the yellow car when the corpse had been dumped in Place de la Concorde.

'I bet,' said Maigret, who had his own thoughts on the matter, 'that we'll find her one of these days in the country.'

It would be hard to overestimate the number of people who, when confronted by some unpleasant problem, suddenly feel an urge to breathe clean country air, usually in a quiet inn where the cooking is good and the wine light-red.

'Shall we take a taxi?'

It would mean more trouble with the clerk in accounts, who always showed a disagreeable tendency to trim expenses claims and was only too ready to argue:

'Do I go around in taxis?'

They hailed a cab rather than cross Pont-Neuf and wait for a bus.

'The Cadran, in Rue de Maubeuge.'

A first-rate brasserie, the sort that Maigret liked best, yet to be modernized and with the classic frieze of mirrors round the walls, the dark-red bench-seat covered with imitation leather, white marble-topped tables and, at intervals, round nickel holders for the waiters' damp-cloths. It smelled gloriously of beer and sauerkraut. There were just a few too many people, people in too much of a hurry, laden with luggage, drinking or eating too quickly, shouting impatiently for waiters, and all with one eye on the large luminous face of the station clock.

The owner of the Cadran, who stood by the till, looking dignified, keeping a watchful eye on everything that was going on, was also cast in traditional mould, being short, portly and bald and wearing a loose-fitting suit and spotless fine leather shoes.

'Two sauerkrauts, two beers and the landlord, please.'

'You wish to speak to Monsieur Jean?'

'Yes.'

An ex-café waiter or maybe a retired restaurant head waiter who had managed finally to set up on his own?

'Gentlemen . . .'

'I would like some information, Monsieur Jean. You

used to have working here a waiter called Albert Rochain. He was known as Li'l Albert, I believe.'

'I've heard the name,'

'You never knew him?'

'It was only three years ago that I bought the business. The woman who was on the till at the time, she knew Albert.'

'Are you saying that she doesn't work here any more?'

'She died last December. She'd spent more than forty years behind that till.'

He gestured towards the polished wood cash-desk, behind which a woman of about thirty, with blonde hair, was enthroned.

'What about the waiters?'

'There was one, also getting on a bit, Ernest, but he has retired since then. Went back to his part of the world, which was somewhere in the Dordogne, I believe.'

Monsieur Jean remained standing in front of the two men, who went on eating their sauerkraut, but never missed anything that happened around him.

'Jules! . . . Table twenty-four . . .'

From there he flashed a smile at a customer who was on her way out.

'François! Help Madame with her luggage!'

'Is the former proprietor still alive?'

'He's fitter than you and me.'

'Do you know where I could find him?'

'At his house, of course. He calls in here to see me from time to time. He's bored. He talks about going back into business.'

'Can you let me have his address?'

'Police?' asked Monsieur Jean directly.

'Detective Chief Inspector Maigret.'

'Sorry! I don't know his number. But I can help – he's asked me to lunch two or three times. Are you familiar with Joinville? Do you know the Ile d'Amour, just beyond the bridge? He doesn't live on the island itself but in a house directly opposite the tip. There's a boat-house in front of it. You won't have any trouble finding it.'

It was half past eight when the taxi drew up outside the house. A plaque of white marble with copperplate lettering read: 'Le Nid'. It showed an exotic bird, or something purporting to be an exotic bird, perched on a nest.

'He must have gone to no end of trouble to think of that!' observed Maigret with a smile.

The former owner of the Cadran was actually called Loiseau, Désiré Loiseau.

'He'll be from the north, you'll see, and he'll offer us a glass of very old gin.'

And so it proved. First they encountered a small, dumpy woman, very blonde and very pink, who had to be seen close up before the fine lines under the thick layer of powder became visible.

'Monsieur Loiseau!' she called. 'Someone to see you! . . .'

She was Madame Loiseau. She showed them into the drawing room, which smelled of polish.

Loiseau was fat too, but also tall and broad, taller and broader than Maigret, though that did not prevent him from being as light on his feet as a dancer.

'Do sit down. You too, monsieur . . . ?'

'Inspector Lucas.'

'Really? I knew someone at school who was also called Lucas. I don't suppose you're Belgian, inspector? I am. It hardly needs saying! No, it's true! I don't mind admitting it. It's nothing to be ashamed of. Sweetheart, why don't you get us a drink . . .'

The small glass of gin duly appeared.

'Albert? Of course I remember him. He was a northerner. Actually I seem to think his mother was Belgian too. I was sorry to see him go. You understand, what matters most in our business is keeping cheerful. People who go to a café prefer to see smiling faces. I recall one waiter, for example, a very willing sort, who had I don't know how many kids. He used to lean over customers who'd ordered soda water or a glass of Vichy or anything non-alcoholic and say in a confidential whisper: "Have you got an ulcer too?" He lived and breathed his ulcer. He talked of nothing else. I had to give him his marching orders because people used to get up and sit somewhere else when they saw him coming towards their table.

'Albert was the very opposite. Always ready for a laugh. He used to hum to himself. The way he wore his cap made him look like a juggler, as if he was always enjoying himself, and he had this way of singing out: "The weather's good today!"'

'And he left you to set up on his own account?'

'Somewhere out towards Charenton, yes.'

'Had he been left money?'

'I don't think so. He talked to me about it. I think it's just that he got married.'

'Was that about the time he left you?'

'Yes. Shortly before.'

'Were you invited to the wedding?'

'I would have been if it had been held in Paris, because when I was in business all my employees were like family. But they went off and tied the knot somewhere far out in the sticks, I've forgotten where exactly.'

'Do you think you could remember?'

'No chance. I don't mind telling you, as far as I'm concerned, anywhere south of the Loire is the Midi.'

'Did you meet his wife?'

'He came one day and introduced her. Dark hair, not very good-looking.'

'Did she have a squint?'

'Her eyes weren't quite together, yes. But it wasn't unpleasant. In some people it's off-putting, but in others it doesn't matter that much.'

'Did you know her maiden name?'

'No. I think I remember that she was related to him, a cousin, or something of the sort. They'd always known each other. Albert used to say: "Since you've got to come to it some time or other, better the devil you know." He used to joke about everything. Seems he had no equal when it came to singing. There were customers who told me seriously that he was good enough to go on the halls.

'Can I offer you another glass? As you see, down here it's quiet, maybe too quiet, and one of these fine days I might well go back into the business. Unfortunately good staff like Albert don't grow on trees. Do you know him? Is he making a go of his bar?'

Maigret chose not to tell them that Albert was dead, because he anticipated an hour of sighs and lamentations.

'Do you know if he had any close friends?'

'He was friends with everybody.'

'Did anyone come to meet him after work, for example?'

'No. He used to go to the races a lot. He managed things so that he'd often be free in the afternoon. But he wasn't reckless. He never tried to borrow money from me. He used to bet within his means. If you see him, tell him from me that . . .'

Madame Loiseau, who hadn't opened her mouth once since her husband had appeared, was still smiling the kind of smile that belongs on a wax head in the window of a hairdressing salon.

Another small one? Yes. Especially as the gin was good. Then off they went to join the raid on a street where nobody would be smiling at them.

6.

Two busloads of police had stopped in Rue de Rivoli on the corner of Rue Vieille-du-Temple, and for a moment the silver buttons of the uniformed men had caught the light of the streetlamps. These men had gone to take up their positions, cordoning off a certain number of streets where plainclothed inspectors of the Police Judiciaire were already stationed.

Then, behind the buses, the prison vans formed up in an orderly line. At the corner of Rue du Roi-de-Sicile, a senior police officer was staring at his watch.

In Rue Saint-Antoine, pedestrians, alarmed, turned and hurried away. Inside the area which had been surrounded, a few lighted windows could still be seen. Lights still burned over the doors of cheap hotels, as did the lamp outside the brothel in Rue des Rosiers.

The senior officer, his eyes still fixed on his watch, was counting down the final seconds. At his side, Maigret, in detached mood or perhaps feeling he was in the way, thrust his hands into his pockets and looked elsewhere.

Forty . . . Fifty . . . Sixty . . . Two loud blasts of a whistle, to which other whistles immediately responded. The men in uniform advanced through the streets like skirmishers while the inspectors marched into the disreputable hotels.

As always happens on these occasions, windows opened on all sides; white figures appeared in the gloom, looking alarmed or irritated. Already raised voices could be heard. Already, a policeman could be observed pushing a prostitute he had dug out of a hole in a corner. She was directing foul-mouthed abuse at him.

There was also the sound of the running footsteps of men trying to make a bolt for it as they ducked into dark alleyways, but in vain, for they merely ran into different police cordons.

'Papers!'

Pocket torches were snapped on and lit suspect faces, greasy passports and identity cards. At the windows were some who had seen it all before and knew that they wouldn't be getting back to sleep for a long time, and who watched the raid with interest, as if it were some kind of show.

Most of the prey were already under lock and key at the Préfecture. They hadn't waited for the raid to happen. From the moment a man had been gunned down in their streets late that afternoon, they had sensed it was coming. And as soon as it was dark, shadows had flitted along walls, men carrying battered suitcases or oddly shaped bundles had run straight into the arms of Maigret's men.

Among them were all sorts: an ex-con who had been banned from the area, pimps, forged identity cards, the unavoidable Poles, Italians whose papers were not in order . . .

All of them, trying to look unconcerned, were questioned roughly:

'Where do you think you're going?'

'Moving house.'

'Why?'

Those eyes, anxious or fierce, in the darkness.

'I found a job.'

'Where?'

Some said they were going to their sister's in the north or somewhere near Toulouse.

'Just get in!'

Prison van. A night in the cells, for an identity check. They were mostly sad cases, though few of them had clear consciences.

'Not one Czech so far, sir!' Maigret had been told.

He had remained at his post, smoking his pipe, grim-faced, watching the moving shadows and hearing shouts, hurried footsteps and occasionally the moist thud of a fist on a face.

It was in the cheap hotels that there was most resistance. Their owners and managers hastily got into trousers and skulked scowling in their offices, where almost all of them slept on camp beds. A few tried to offer drinks to the uniformed officers who stood guard in the hall outside while inspectors stamped up the stairs to the floors above.

There, the reeking hotel cells sprang into teeming life. Knuckles sounded on a door:

'Police!'

People in night clothes, men and women still half asleep, whey-faced, and all with that same anxious, sometimes haggard, look.

'Papers!'

Barefooted they fetched them from under pillows or from drawers, sometimes having to rummage through ancient, old-fashioned trunks which had originated on the other side of Europe.

In the Hôtel du Lion d'Or, a naked man remained seated on his bed, swinging his legs, while the woman with him showed her prostitute's registration card.

'What about you?'

He looked at the inspector uncomprehendingly.

'Passport!'

He still did not move. His body looked all the paler for being covered with very dark, very long hair. People from neighbouring rooms looked in and laughed.

'Who is this man?' the inspector asked the woman.

'Don't know.'

'Didn't he say anything to you?'

'He doesn't speak a word of French.'

'Where did you pick him up?'

'In the street.'

One for the Préfecture lock-up! His clothes were thrust into his hand and hand gestures were used to order him to put them on. It look him some time to understand what was expected of him. He kept protesting and turning to the woman, apparently asking her for something. His money back, possibly? Perhaps he had arrived in Paris no later than that same evening and now he would end his first night in the cells in Quai de l'Horloge.

'Papers!'

Doors opened on to decaying rooms each exuding, in addition to the general fetid smell of the establishment, the particular odour of the transients who paid by the week or the night. Fifteen, maybe a score of people formed a group at the head of the line of prison vans. They were bundled inside them one by one, and some of the women, who knew the drill, joked with the policemen. One, for a laugh, made obscene gestures in their direction.

Some were in tears while some of the men clenched their fists, among them being a very blond adolescent with a shaved head who had no papers at all and had been found in possession of a revolver.

Both inside the hotels and out in the streets there was a preliminary triage. The screening proper would be done at the Préfecture, either during the night or the next morning.

'Papers.'

The hotel-keepers were the most apprehensive because they might lose their licences, as none of them was fully compliant with the law. Under their roofs were clients who were not signed in.

'As you know, inspector, my paperwork's always been in order, but when someone turns up at midnight and you're half asleep . . .'

An upstairs window of the Hôtel du Lion d'Or opened. The milky globe over its door was the one closest to Maigret. There was a blast of a police whistle. He stepped forwards and tilted his head back.

'What is it?'

As it happened, the inspector on duty who looked down at him was very young. He stammered:

'Detective Chief Inspector, I think you should come up.'

Closely followed by Lucas, Maigret started up the narrow staircase where they brushed against the wall and banister at the same time. The stairs creaked. All these buildings ought to have been knocked down decades, if not centuries ago, or rather burned down along with their colonies of fleas and lice from every country on earth.

It was on the second floor. A door was open. A low-watt light bulb with no shade and yellow filaments burned at the end of its flex. The room was empty. It contained two iron bedsteads, of which only one had been slept in. There was also a mattress on the floor, blankets made of coarse grey wool, a jacket on a chair, a primus stove and various foodstuffs and empty litre bottles on a table.

'Through here, sir . . .'

The door communicating with the next room was open, and Maigret saw a woman lying on a bed, a face on a pillow and two brown, burning, magnificent eyes which glared at him fiercely.

'What's the problem?' he asked.

Rarely had he seen such an expressive face. And never one so wild.

'Take a closer look at her,' stuttered the young officer. 'I tried to make her get up. I talked to her but she couldn't be bothered to answer. So I went closer to the bed and tried to shake her by the shoulders. Look at my hand. She bit me and drew blood.'

The woman did not smile when she saw the officer show his painful thumb. On the contrary, she screwed up her face as if she had suddenly been struck by a terrible pain.

Maigret, who was looking at the bed, frowned and growled:

'She's having a baby!'

He turned to Lucas.

'Phone for an ambulance. Tell them to take her to the maternity ward. Then tell the owner to come up at once.'

The young officer was now all blushes and did not dare look at the bed. The search continued on the other storeys of the building. The floorboards shook.

'Don't want to say anything?' Maigret asked the woman. 'Don't you understand French?'

She was still glaring at him. It was quite impossible to guess what she was thinking. The only emotion on her face was intense hatred.

She was young. She was probably not yet twenty-five, and her full cheeks were framed by long, glossy, black hair. The stairs became congested. The hotel-keeper came to an uncertain stop in the doorway.

'Who's this?'

'She's called Maria.'

'Maria who?'

'I don't think she's got another name.'

Suddenly Maigret felt very angry and immediately regretted it. He picked up a man's shoe from under the foot of the bed.

'What's this?' he cried throwing it at the hotel-keeper's feet. 'Doesn't that have a name either? . . . Or this? . . . Or this? . . .'

He fished a jacket and a dirty shirt from the back of a cupboard, together with another shoe and a cap.

'Or these?'

He went back into the room next door and pointed to two suitcases in a corner.

'And that?'

A piece of cheese on greaseproof paper, glasses – four of them – plates on which there were still a few slices of salami.

'Did everyone who lived here sign your register? Well? Speak up? And start by telling me how many of them there were.'

'I don't know.'

'Does this woman speak French?'

'I don't know . . . No . . . She just understands a few words.'

'How long has she been here?'

'I don't know.'

He had a nasty bluish boil on his neck, a sickly look and thinning hair. He had not fastened his braces, so that his trousers kept slipping down his thighs, and he was obliged to hold them up with both hands.

'When did all this start?'

Maigret pointed to the woman.

'No one told me . . .'

'You're lying . . . And what about the others? Where are they?'

'They're probably gone.'

'When?'

Maigret walked towards him, fists bunched. At that moment he'd got to the point where he could have hit the man . . .

'They ran away immediately after that man was shot in the street, didn't they? They were a lot smarter than all the others! They didn't hang around waiting for the police cordon to be set up.'

No answer.

'Take a look at this. You recognize him, don't you?'

He thrust the photo of Victor Poliensky under his nose.'

'Do you recognize him?'

'Yes.'

'Did he live in this room?'

'Next door.'

'With the others? . . . And which of them slept with the woman?'

'I swear I don't know. Maybe more than one of them . . .'

Lucas was back. Almost simultaneously there was the sound outside of an ambulance siren. The woman screamed with pain but bit her lip and glared defiantly at the men.

'Listen, Lucas, I'm going to have to stay here for some time yet. I want you to go with her. Don't leave her side, by which I mean that you're not to stray from her ward in the hospital. As soon as I can I'll try to dig out a Czech interpreter for you.'

Other tenants who were being led away and were walking glumly down the stairs bumped into the ambulance men, who were on their way up with a stretcher. In the dim light, there was something unearthly about the whole scene. It looked like a nightmare, a nightmare which was filled with the reek of dirt and sweat.

Maigret preferred to move into the other room while the ambulance men were taking care of the young woman.

'Where will you take her?' he asked Lucas.

'Laennec. I had to phone round three hospitals before I found a bed for her.'

The hotel-keeper did not dare move but stared lugubriously at the floor.

'Stay here! And close the door!' Maigret barked at him when the field was clear. 'Now, tell me everything.'

'I don't know much, I swear.'

'Earlier on, an inspector came and showed you a photo. Is that right?'

'It is.'

'You said you didn't know the man.'

'Not quite. I said he wasn't staying in the hotel.'

'How do you mean?'

'He's not in the register, nor the woman either. Somebody else is signed in for both rooms.'

'Since when?'

'About five months.'

'What's his name?'

'Serge Madok.'

'Is he the leader?'

'Leader of what?'

'Let me give you a piece of advice. Don't be stupid! Otherwise we'll carry on this little chat elsewhere, and tomorrow morning this place will be closed down. Have you got that?'

'I've always been above board . . .'

'Except tonight. Tell me about Serge Madok. Is he Czech?'

'That's what it says on his papers. They all talk the same lingo. It's not Polish. I'm used to Poles.'

'Age?'

'About thirty. At the start, he told me he worked in a factory.'

'Did he really have a job?'

'No.'

'How do you know?'

'Because he was here all day.'

'How about the others?'

'The others likewise. There was only ever one who went out. Most often it was the woman who used to go down to the market in Rue Saint-Antoine.'

'What did they do all day?'

'Nothing. They slept, ate, drank, played cards . . . They were no trouble. Now and then, they'd start singing, but never at night, so there was nothing I could say.'

'How many of them were there?'

'Four men and Maria.'

'And did the four men . . . with Maria?'

'I don't know.'

'You're lying! Tell me!'

'There was something going on all right, but what, I couldn't exactly say. Sometimes they quarrelled, and I got the feeling it was about her. Several times I walked into the back room, and it wasn't always the same man who was missing.'

'What about the one in the photo, Victor Poliensky?'

'I think so. It could have been him. In any case, he was in love.'

'Which of them was the most important?'

'I think it was the one they called Carl. I did hear them say his other name, but it's such a mouthful that I could never pronounce it, and it didn't stick in my mind.'

'Wait a moment.'

From his pocket Maigret took his memo-pad like the one laundresses use and licked the end of his pencil the way schoolchildren do.

'First, the woman, whom you call Maria. Then Carl. Plus Serge Madok, in whose name both rooms were let. And Victor Poliensky, the one who was shot. Is that the lot?'

'There's the kid.'

'What kid?'

'I assume he's Maria's brother. Anyway, he looks like her. I always heard him called Pietr. He must be sixteen or seventeen.'

'And he didn't work either?'

The hotel-keeper shook his head. As Maigret had opened the window to ventilate the rooms – though the air from the street made the place smell as foul as the air inside the hotel – he was cold, without a jacket, and was beginning to shiver.

'None of them's got a job.'

'Yet they spent a lot of money?'

Maigret nodded towards the pile of empty wine bottles in a corner, among which were a number of champagne bottles.

'By local standards, they spent a lot, but it wasn't regular. There were times when they had to tighten their belts. It was pretty obvious. When the kid made several trips out with empty bottles to get the money back on them, it meant funds were running low.'

'Didn't anybody ever come to see them?'

'Might have done.'

'You still want to go on with this conversation down at Quai des Orfèvres?'

'No. I'll tell you everything I know. Someone did come to see them. Two or three times.'

'Who?'

'A gent. Very well dressed.'

'Did he go up to their room? What did he say when he called in at your office?'

'He never asked me anything. He must have known which floor they were on. He went straight up.'

'Is that all?'

The noise outside had gradually abated. Lighted windows grew dark. There was still the sound of footsteps as a few inspectors made their rounds, ringing the last doorbells.

The senior police officer climbed the stairs.

'What are you orders now, sir? It's all over. Both vans are full.'

'They can go. Will you ask two of my inspectors to come up here?'

The hotel-keeper moaned:

'I'm freezing.'

'And I'm too hot.'

That was because he had no wish to put his overcoat down anywhere in that filthy hole.

'This man who came to see them, did you ever run across him anywhere else? Did you ever see his picture in the papers? Was it this man?'

He showed him the photo of Li'l Albert which he still had in his pocket.

'That doesn't look like him. This other one was a good-looking man, very well dressed, with a small brown moustache.'

'How old?'

'Maybe thirty-five? I noticed he wore a great big gold ring.'

'French? Czech?'

'Definitely not French. He talked to them in their lingo.'

'Did you listen outside the door?'

'I do sometimes. I like to know what goes on in my place, see.'

'Especially since it didn't take long for the penny to drop.'

'Drop about what?'

'You think I'm a fool, don't you? What do men who hide up in holes like this place and never go looking for work do? What do they live on? Answer me!'

'It's nothing to do with me.'

'How often did they all go out together?'

The hotel-keeper turned red, hesitated, but then the way Maigret was staring at him convinced him that a measure of truthfulness would be in order.

'Four, maybe five times.'

'How long were they gone for? A whole night?'

'What makes you think it was at night? It was usually at night, yes. But once they stayed away two days and two nights. I had even started thinking they weren't coming back.'

'You thought they'd been arrested, didn't you?'

'Maybe.'

'What did they give you when they got back?'

'They paid their rent.'

'The rent for one person? Because actually there was only one person's name in your register.'

'They gave me a bit extra.'

'How much? Have a care, friend. Don't forget I can put you behind bars for aiding and abetting.'

'Once they gave me five hundred francs. Another time two thousand.'

'And then they lived it up.'

'Yes. They went straight out and bought a lot of stuff to eat and drink.'

'Which of them stayed on guard?'

This time, the hotel-keeper looked even more uneasy and he automatically glanced round at the door.

'There are two exits to this place, is that right?'

'Well, if you go through the back yards by jumping over a couple of walls, you come out in Rue Vieille-du-Temple.'

'Who was on guard?'

'In the street?'

'Yes, in the street. And I assume there was always one

looking out of the window? When Madok asked for a room, he asked for one that overlooked the street, didn't he?'

'Yes. It's also a true that one of them was always hanging around on the pavement outside. They took turns.'

'Another question: which of them threatened to sort you out if you talked?'

'Carl.'

'When was this?'

'The first time they came back after being out all night.'

'How did you know that the threat was serious, that they were capable of killing?'

'I walked into the room. I often do my rounds but say I'm just checking to see if the electricity is working or that they've changed the sheets.'

'Do they change them often?'

'Every month. Once I caught the woman washing a shirt in the wash-basin and saw there was blood on it.'

'Whose shirt was it?'

'One of the men's, I don't know which . . .'

Two inspectors were outside on the landing, waiting until Maigret got round to giving them instructions.

'I want one of you to phone Moers. He's probably asleep by now unless he's finishing off some piece of work. If he's not at the office, call him at home. I want him to come here with his gear.'

Ignoring the hotel-keeper, he wandered through both rooms, opening a cupboard here, a drawer there and kicking a pile of dirty washing left on the floor. The paper on the walls had faded and was peeling off in places. The beds were dirty and uninviting, and the blankets the same unpleasant grey as the ones in soldiers' barracks. Everything was in a mess. When they fled, the occupants had clearly gathered up what was most valuable but had not dared take anything bulky with them for fear of drawing attention to themselves.

'Did they leave immediately after the shot was fired?' asked Maigret.

'Straight away.'

'Through the front door?'

'No, through the yards . . .'

'Which one was outside at that moment?'

'Victor, of course. And Serge Madok.'

'Which one came down to answer the phone?'

'How do you know anyone phoned?'

'Answer me!'

'There was a call for them at about half past four, you're right. I didn't recognize the voice, but whoever it was spoke their lingo. All he said was Carl's name. I told him he was wanted. He came down. I can see him now in my office. He was livid and waved his hands about furiously. He yelled down the phone. When he went back upstairs, he started swearing like a trooper again. Then, after no time at all, Madok came down.'

'So it was Madok who killed his friend?'

'It's very likely.'

'Did they try to take the woman with them?'

'I asked them about that when they were passing through the hall. I thought that it would all mean big trouble for me. I would have preferred it if they'd all just cleared out. I didn't know she was going to have her kid so soon. I went up and told her to get out like the rest of them. She was in bed. She just stared at me cool as anything. You know, she understands more French than she lets on. She didn't bother to say anything but suddenly she doubled up with pain, and I got the message.'

'Listen,' said Maigret to the officer who was still there, 'I want you to stay and wait for Moers. Don't let anybody into these two rooms, especially not this clown. Are you armed?'

The officer patted the revolver, which made a bulge in the pocket of his jacket.

'Get Moers to look for fingerprints first. Then tell him to take away anything that might give us a lead. It's obvious they didn't leave anything in the way of written paper or documents behind them. I've checked.'

Old socks, underpants, a harmonica, a box containing needle and thread, various garments, several packs of playing cards, small figures carved with a knife from soft wood . . .

Telling the hotel-keeper to go first, he followed him down the stairs. What was called the 'office' was a tiny room, badly lit, with no ventilation, which contained a camp bed and a table on which there was a primus stove and the remains of a meal.

'I don't suppose you kept a note of the dates when the villains went out on the prowl?'

The man replied with an instant 'no'.

'I thought not. Still, no matter. You have until tomorrow morning to remember. Got that? Tomorrow morning

I'll be here or have you brought to me in my office. I'll expect dates, listen carefully, *precise dates*. If I don't get them I will regretfully be forced to arrest you.'

There was still something else that the hotel-keeper wanted to say but he hesitated . . .

'If by any chance, somebody came here . . . will you . . . will you authorize me to use my revolver?'

'So you're thinking you know far too much, right? And that it might occur to them to do to you what they did to Victor?'

'I'm scared.'

'There'll be a policeman permanently on duty in the street outside.'

'What if they come the other way, through the yards at the back?'

'I hadn't forgotten. I'll post another man to stand guard in Rue Vieille-du-Temple.'

The streets were empty, and the silence was a surprise after all the turmoil of the last few hours. There was no sign now of the raid. No windows were lit. Their occupants were all asleep except those who had been carted off to the Préfecture and Maria, who must now be having her baby in hospital while Lucas paced up and down outside her door.

He posted the two men as promised and gave them detailed instructions. He then had to stand for a considerable time while he waited for a taxi in Rue de Rivoli. The night was clear and cool.

As he got into the cab, he hesitated. He hadn't slept the previous night. But he had rested up for three whole days and three whole nights while he nursed his attack of bronchitis. Did Moers have time to sleep?

'Where can we find some place that's still open?' he asked.

He felt suddenly hungry. Hungry and thirsty. The thought of very cold beer, with a silvery, frothing head on it, made his mouth water.

'Apart from the nightclubs, I can only think of the Coupole or the small bars around Les Halles.'

He knew all that. So why had he asked the question?

'Make it the Coupole.'

The main dining room was shut, but the bar was still open and contained a few, somnolent customers. He ordered two magnificent ham sandwiches and drank three beers one after the other. He had kept the taxi waiting. It was four in the morning.

'Quai des Orfèvres.'

On the way, he changed his mind.

'Take me instead to the police cells on Quai de l'Horloge.'

Everyone was there and the smell reminded him of Rue du Roi-de-Sicile. The men had been lined up on one side, the women on the other, along with all the down-and-outs, drunks and registered prostitutes rounded up in Paris that night.

Some were lying on the floor, asleep. The regulars had taken their shoes off and were massaging their painful feet. Through the bars, women joked with the custody officers, and sometimes one of them would lift her skirts up to her waist as a gesture of defiance.

The duty officers played cards around a stove on which a coffee-pot had been put to boil. Inspectors were waiting for orders from Maigret.

In theory it wasn't until eight o'clock that the identity papers of everyone who had been rounded would be checked prior to the detainees being sent upstairs, where they would be stripped for the medical examination and biometrics.

'You might as well make a start now. Leave checking their papers to the day superintendent. I want you to question all those picked up in Rue du Roi-de-Sicile one by one, especially the women . . . And most particularly any males and females who live in the Hôtel du Lion d'Or, if there are any . . .'

'One woman and two men.'

'Right. Get them to tell all they know about the Czechs and Maria . . .'

He gave them brief descriptions of the members of the gang, and then the officers sat down at separate tables.

The questioning, which would last for the rest of the night, got under way just as Maigret walked back to his office through the dark corridors of the Palais de Justice, groping for light switches as he went.

Joseph, the night clerk, stood up when he appeared, and it was good to see that cheerful face again. The light was on in the inspectors' office, where, as it happened, a phone began to ring.

Maigret walked in. Bodin was talking into the phone and was saying:

'I'll put him on . . . He's just come in . . .'

It was Lucas who informed Maigret that Maria had had a boy. Nine pounds. She had almost leaped out of bed when she saw the nurse leaving the room with the baby to clean it up.

7.

When he got out of the taxi which dropped him at Laennec Hospital in Rue de Sèvres, Maigret noticed a large car with a diplomatic number plate. At the main door, a tall, thin man was waiting. His clothes were so impeccable, his every movement so carefully studied and his facial expressions so exquisite that, rather than listen to his carefully articulated words, you simply felt like standing back to watch the spectacle.

Yet he was not even the lowliest under-secretary in the Czechoslovakian embassy, simply a minor official.

'His Excellency has asked me . . .'

Maigret, who reckoned that the last few hours were some of the busiest he had ever known, decided to preempt the formalities and growled:

'Yes, of course . . .'

Still, as they went up the stairs in the hospital, he did turn and ask a question. It made the man start:

'I imagine you speak Czech?'

Lucas was in the corridor, leaning on his elbows, gloomily staring out at the gardens through a window. The sky that morning was grey, and it was raining. A nurse had approached him and asked him not to smoke, and he now gave a sigh and pointed at Maigret's pipe:

'You'll be told to put it out, sir.'

They had to wait until the duty nurse came to collect them. She was middle-aged and totally impervious to Maigret's reputation and made it plain that there was no love lost between her and the police.

'You mustn't tire her. When I let you know that it's time to leave, I would ask you not to try to stay any longer.'

Maigret shrugged and was first through the door and into the small white room, where Maria seemed to be dozing while her baby lay fast asleep in a cot by the side of the bed. But the look which escaped through the woman's half-closed eyelids did not miss a single move the two men made.

She was as beautiful as she had been last night in Rue du Roi-de-Sicile. Her face was paler. Her hair had been done up in two thick plaits which coiled round her head.

After putting his hat down on a chair, Maigret said to the Czech:

'Please ask her what her name is.'

He waited with no great hopes. He was right: the young woman merely glared with eyes full of hate at the man who was speaking to her in her own language.

'She won't answer,' said the interpreter. 'As far as I can judge, she isn't Czech but Slovak. I have spoken to her in both languages and it was when I used the second that there was a reaction.'

'Perhaps you would be good enough to explain that I urge her very strongly to answer my questions. If she doesn't, then despite her condition, she could – now, today – be transferred to the infirmary in the Santé prison.'

The Czech swallowed hard, as any offended gentleman

might, and the nurse who was lingering in the room muttered as if to herself:

'That I would like to see!'

Then she spoke directly to Maigret:

'Didn't you see the sign at the foot of the stairs saying that smoking is not allowed?'

With unexpected meekness, Maigret took the pipe from his mouth and held it between his fingers while it went out.

Meantime, Maria had said a few words.

'Would you translate, please?'

'She says that she doesn't care what you do and that she hates us all. I was right. She's Slovakian, probably from southern Slovakia. A country woman.'

He seemed somehow relieved. His honour as a pure Czech from Prague had not been at stake since they were dealing with a mere Slovakian peasant.

Maigret had taken his memo-pad from his pocket.

'Ask her where she was on the night of 12 and 13 October last.'

This time, the question struck home, her expression darkened, and her eyes turned more insistently on the inspector. But no sound came from her lips.

'And now the same question for the night of 8 and 9 December.'

She became agitated. Her chest heaved visibly, and she made an involuntary movement towards the cot, as if she wanted to take hold of her baby and protect him.

She was a magnificent woman. Only the nurse could not see that she belonged to a different order from the rest of them and thus was able to treat her just like any other woman, as a patient who had just had a baby.

'Will you soon be done asking her all these asinine questions?'

'If that's what you think, I'll ask her another question which might make you change your mind, mademoiselle . . . or is it madame?'

'It's mademoiselle, if you don't mind.'

'I thought as much.'

He turned to the interpreter.

'Would you translate, please. During the night of 8 and 9 December, at a farm in Picardy, at Saint-Gilles-les-Vaudreuves, an entire family was brutally slaughtered with an axe. On the night of 12 and 13 October, two old men, both farmers, were killed in the same way at their farm at Saint-Aubin, also in Picardy. During the night of 21 and 22 November, two elderly men and their simple-minded farm hand had already been attacked, also with an axe . . .'

'I assume you are going to claim that she did it?'

'One moment, mademoiselle. Would you kindly allow the interpreter . . .'

The Czech translated with evident distaste, as though merely speaking of these massacres dirtied his hands. On hearing the first words, the woman half sat up in the bed, exposing one breast, which she did not attempt to hide.

'Until 8 December, nothing was known about the murderers because they left no survivors behind. Are you following, mademoiselle?'

'I believe the doctor authorized a visit of just a few minutes only . . .'

'Don't worry. She's tough. Just look at her.'

She was still beautiful poised next to her son like a she-wolf, like a lioness, as beautiful as she must have been leading her men.

'Translate word for word, please. On 8 December, there was an oversight. A little girl, nine years old, in bare feet, wearing her nightdress, managed to slip out of bed before they got round to her and hid in a corner where no one thought of searching. She saw everything and heard everything. She saw a young woman with dark hair, a magnificent, wild woman holding the flame of a candle to her mother's feet while one of the men split her grandfather's skull and another poured a drink for his companions. The farmer's wife screamed, begged, writhed in agony while this . . .'

He nodded towards the woman who had just had a baby.

'. . . this woman smiled, ratcheted up the torture by stubbing out a lighted cigarette on her breasts.'

'Really!' protested the nurse.

'Translate!'

While this was going on, he observed Maria, who never took her eyes off him, withdrew into herself, eyes blazing.

'Ask her if she has anything to say for herself.'

All they got was a disdainful smile.

'The little girl who escaped the carnage is now an orphan. She is being looked after by a family in Amiens. This morning, she was shown a photograph of this woman which was telegraphed by belinogram. She formally identified her. She had not been told anything in advance. The photo was simply placed in front of her, and her reaction was so violent that she suffered a nervous collapse. Since you're Czech, monsieur, please translate.'

'She's Slovak,' he repeated.

At this point, the baby started to cry, and the nurse, after looking at her watch, lifted him out of his cot. While she changed him, the mother did not take her eyes off her.

'I must point out, Detective Chief Inspector, that your time is up.'

'Was time up too for the poor people I've been talking about?'

'The baby must be put to the breast.'

'Please see to it.'

It was the very first time that Maigret had conducted such an interview while a new-born baby fastened its lips to the white breast of a murderess.

'Still not answering, is she? I imagine she won't say anything either when you ask her about Madame Rival, who was murdered like the others on her farm on 19 January. She's the latest to date. Her daughter, aged forty, also died. I'm assuming Maria was there. As usual, recent burn marks were found on her body. Translate.'

All around him he was aware of a feeling of deep unease, of muted hostility, but he did not care. He was exhausted. If he had been able to sit in a chair for just five minutes, he would have gone to sleep.

'Now ask her about her confederates, her men, about Victor Poliensky, a kind of village idiot as strong as a gorilla, Serge Madok, who has a thick neck and greasy skin, about Carl and the kid they call Pietr.'

She picked up on the names as Maigret pronounced them and with each mention she flinched.

'Did she also go to bed with the kid?'

'Do you want me to translate?'

'Please. I don't think you could say anything that would bring a blush to her cheek.'

Backed into a corner, she still managed to raise a smile when she heard the name of the adolescent.

'Ask if he really is her brother.'

Curiously enough there were moments when an expression of genuine tenderness flickered in the woman's eyes and not only when she held the face of her baby close to her breast.

'And now, Monsieur . . .'

'My name is Franz Lehel.'

'I couldn't care less. I would be grateful if you would translate what I am about to say very accurately, word by word. It is possible that the life of your compatriot could depend on it. Tell her first that her life depends on the attitude she chooses to adopt.'

'Must I really?'

And the nurse murmured:

'It's a disgrace!'

But Maria did not turn a hair. She just turned a little paler but still managed a smile.

'There is another man. We don't know who he is but he's their leader.'

'Shall I translate?'

'Please do.'

This time what they got from the woman was a sarcastic grin.

'She won't talk, I know. I was expecting it when I got here. She isn't the kind of woman who is easily intimidated. Still, there is one detail I would like to clear up, because people's lives are at stake.'

'Shall I translate?'

'Why did I ask you to come here?'

'To translate. I'm sorry.'

He spoke very stiffly, like a schoolboy reciting a lesson learned by rote.

'From 12 October to 21 November is about six weeks. From 21 November to 8 December is a little more than a fortnight. It's another six weeks to 19 January. Don't you get it? Those are the periods, more or less, that it took for the gang to spend the money they stole. It is now the end of February . . . I can't promise anything. When the case comes to trial, others will decide what her fate will be. Translate.'

'Would you repeat the dates?'

Maigret repeated them and waited.

'Add now that if, by answering my final questions, she prevents further massacres taking place, due account will be taken of the fact.'

She did not react, but the scowl on her face turned to an expression of contempt.

'I'm not asking her to tell me where her friends are now. I'm not even asking her to tell me the name of their leader. I want to know if their funds are running low and if they're planning a job for the next few days.'

The only effect was to light up Maria's eyes.

'Very well. She won't answer. I think I've got the message. All that remains now is to find out if Victor Poliensky was the killer.'

She listened closely to the interpreter, then waited. Maigret was getting tired of having to keep going through the man from the embassy.

'It's likely that not more than one of them is handy with an axe. If that wasn't Victor's role, I don't see why the gang would have bothered to drag a halfwit around with them. It was he ultimately who led us to Maria's arrest, and he will lead us to the rest of them.'

The interpreter was speaking again. For the moment, Maria seemed to be winning the battle. They knew nothing. She was the only one who knew everything. She was in bed, physically weakened, with an infant hanging on her breast, but she had stayed silent and would maintain her silence.

An involuntary glance out of the window provided the clue to what she was really thinking. When they had left her behind in Rue du Roi-de-Sicile – and it was probably she who had insisted they abandon her – they must have made certain promises.

She knew the men around her. She trusted them. As long as they remained at large, she ran no risks. They would come for her. Sooner or later, they would get her out of this place, or at a later stage even out of the infirmary inside the Santé prison.

She was superb. Her nostrils flared. An inscrutable smile

lingered on her full lips. She was not made of the same stuff as these people around her nor even her men. They had chosen once and for all to live on the margins. They were wild beasts, and the bleating of sheep touched off no spark of compassion in them.

Where, in what lower depths, in what world of poverty had their group been formed? They had all been hungry. It was very evident that once they had pulled a job, all they thought about was eating, eating all day, eating and drinking, sleeping, making love then eating again, oblivious both to their run-down surroundings in Rue du Roi-de-Sicile and to their threadbare clothes, which were little better than rags.

They did not kill for money. To them, money was merely something that enabled them to eat and drink without a care, in their little corner, indifferent to the rest of humankind.

She was not even interested in her appearance. The dresses found in her room were cheap frocks like the ones she had worn in her village back home. She did not use face-powder or lipstick. She did not own expensive underwear. Given the way they were and behaved, they would in earlier times or other climes have lived exactly the same lives, naked, in forest or jungle.

'Tell her that I'll be back and that I ask her to reflect. She has a child now . . .'

He lowered his voice involuntarily as he said these last words.

'We'll leave you to it for now,' he said to the nurse. 'I shall send you a second inspector shortly. I'll phone

Dr Boucard. It is Dr Boucard who is looking after her, isn't it?'

'He's the head of department.'

'If she can be moved, she will be probably transferred to the Santé either this evening or tomorrow morning.'

Despite everything he had revealed to her about her patient, she still regarded him with resentment.

'Goodbye, mademoiselle. Come, monsieur.'

In the corridor outside he had a few words with Lucas, who knew nothing of recent developments.

The nurse who had escorted them up from the ground floor stood waiting for them a little further along. Outside a door were five or six vases full of fresh-cut flowers.

'Whose are these?' he asked.

The nurse was young and blonde, and plump in her uniform.

'They're nobody's now. The lady who was in the room has just this minute gone home. She left the flowers. She had lots of friends.'

He spoke quietly to her. She said yes. She looked surprised. But the Czech would have been even more surprised had he guessed what Maigret had just done.

He had just said, in a slightly awkward voice:

'Would you put some of them in room twenty-one?'

Because the room was bare and cold, because after all there was a woman in it and a new-born child.

It was eleven thirty. In the long, dimly lit corridor lined with the offices of the examining magistrates, a few men, handcuffed and tieless, flanked by guards, were still sitting on backless benches waiting for their turn. There were women too, witnesses who were growing impatient. Monsieur Coméliau, looking grimmer and more care-worn than ever, had been obliged to ask a colleague to lend him additional chairs and had packed his clerk off to lunch. At Maigret's behest, the commissioner of the Police Judiciaire was present. He was sitting in an armchair while the seat generally reserved for suspects who were being interviewed was occupied by Detective Chief Inspector Colombani of the Sûreté.

In theory, the Police Judiciaire has responsibility for only Central and Greater Paris. But for the last five months, in conjunction with other flying squads, Colombani had been leading an investigation into the case of the 'Picardy Killers', as the newspapers had called them after the first crime had been reported.

Early that morning, he had had a meeting with Maigret and had given him everything he had on the case.

Early too, just before nine o'clock, one of the inspectors assigned to Rue du Roi-de-Sicile had knocked on Maigret's door.

'He's here,' he had said.

The man in question was the owner of the Hôtel du Lion d'Or. He had thought things over during the night, or rather the last part of the night. Gaunt, ill-shaven, his clothes creased, he had approached the inspector as he paced up and down in the street outside.

'I want to go to Quai des Orfèvres,' he had said.

'Go ahead.'

'I'm scared.'

'I'll walk with you.'

But hadn't Victor been mown down in the middle of a street crowded with people?

'I'd rather we went by taxi. I'll pay.'

When he walked into the office, Maigret had his file open on the desk in front of him. The man had three convictions to his name.

'Have you got those dates?'

'I've been thinking about it, yes. We'll have to see how it goes. The minute you promise me police protection . . .'

He stank of cowardice and sickness. He made you think of some contagious disease. Yet this was the man who had been arrested on two separate occasions and charged with indecent assault.

'The first time they went out I didn't pay much attention, but the second time I took notice.'

'The second time? You mean 21 November?'

'How do you know that?'

'Because I've been thinking about it too and reading the papers.'

'I had half a thought it was them, but I didn't show I suspected anything.'

'But they guessed anyway, didn't they?'

'I don't know. They gave me a thousand-franc note.'

'Yesterday you said it was five hundred.'

'I made a mistake. It was the next time, when they got back, that Carl threatened me . . .'

'Did they used to go off in a car?'

'I don't know. Either way, they always left my place on foot.'

'Did the visits from the other man, the one whose name you don't know, occur just a few days before?'

'Now that I think about it, I believe they did.'

'Did he sleep with Maria too?'

'No.'

'Now I want you, in your own time, to come clean about something. Think back to your first two convictions.'

'I was just young . . .'

'That makes it even more disgusting. I know you: Maria must have given you ideas . . .'

'I never touched her!'

'I bet you didn't! You were too scared of the others.'

'And of her too.'

'Good! Now at least you're being honest. Except that going up and opening their door from time to time wasn't enough, was it?'

'I made a hole in the wall. It's true. I fixed it so that the room next door was occupied as little as possible.'

'Who slept with her?'

'They all did.'

'Including the kid?'

'Especially the kid.'

'Yesterday you told me that he was probably her brother.'

'Because he looks like her. He was the most in love with her. I saw him crying several times. When he was with her, he used to beg her . . .'

'To do what?'

'I don't know. They never spoke French. When one of the others was in her room, he would sometimes come down and go out and get drunk all by himself in a small bar in Rue des Rosiers.'

'Did they argue amongst themselves?'

'The men didn't like each other.'

'And you really don't know whose was the shirt with blood on it that you saw being rinsed through in the wash-basin?'

'I'm not sure. I saw Victor wearing it. But they some-times wore each other's clothes.'

'In your opinion, of all of them who lived in your hotel, which one was the leader?'

'They didn't have a leader. When they'd start fighting, Maria would bawl them out and they'd stop.'

Then the hotelier had gone back to his squalid estab-lishment, escorted once more by an inspector, to whom he clung fearfully in the street, his skin clammy with the sweat of terror. It is likely that he was even more malo-dorous than usual, because fear has a smell.

And now, Coméliau, in his starched detachable collar, dark tie and immaculate suit, had his eyes fixed on Maigret, who was sitting on the window-sill, with his back to the courtyard outside.

'The woman hasn't said anything and will go on refus-ing to talk,' said the inspector as he puffed calmly on his pipe. 'Since yesterday evening, we've had three wild ani-mals on the loose in Paris, Serge Madok, Carl and the kid Pietr, who, despite his age, is unlikely to be some angelic choirboy. And that's not including the man who paid them visits and is probably the brains behind the whole gang.'

'I take it,' broke in the examining magistrate, 'that you have done the necessary?'

He would have dearly liked to catch Maigret out. Maigret had learned too much too quickly and too easily. While seeming to be focusing entirely on his dead man, on Li'l Albert, he had in fact smoked out a gang the police had been hunting without success for five months.

'You can set your mind at rest on that score. All the mainline railway stations have been alerted. It won't help, but it's routine. Roads and frontiers are being watched. All by the book. Memos have been circulated, telegrams sent and phone calls made, and thousands of men have been mobilized, but . . .'

'It's all vital . . .'

'Which is why it was done. We're also keeping a watch on cheap hotels and boarding houses, especially those similar to the Lion d'Or. These men must be holed up somewhere.'

'A newspaper proprietor who happens to be a friend of mine phoned me earlier to complain about you. It seems you are refusing to tell reporters anything about what's going on.'

'Perfectly correct. I think it would serve no purpose to inform the population of Paris that we are looking for several killers who are currently loose on the city streets.'

'I agree with Maigret,' said the commissioner of the Police Judiciaire.

'I am not criticizing anybody, gentlemen. I am merely trying to form a view. You all have your own methods. Maigret in particular has his own methods, which are sometimes quite distinctive. He does not always seem keen to keep me informed even though ultimately I have full responsibility. At my request, the public prosecutor has just brought together the case of the Picardy gang and the investigation of the murder of Albert. I would like to know exactly where we are with it.'

'We already know,' intoned Maigret in a pointedly monotonous voice, 'how the victims were chosen.'

'Have you had witness statements from northern colleagues?'

'We didn't need them. Moers found plenty of fingerprints in the two rooms in Rue du Roi-de-Sicile. When the gang broke into the farmhouses, they wore rubber gloves and left no traces behind them. Whoever murdered Li'l Albert also wore gloves. But the men who lived at the Lion d'Or wore nothing on their hands. Criminal Records has come up with a match for just one of them.'

'Which one?'

'Carl. His full name is Carl Lipschitz. He was born in Bohemia and arrived in France legally five years ago on a perfectly valid passport. He was part of a group of agricultural labourers who were sent out to work on large farms in Picardy and Artois.'

'For what reason were his details entered in the criminal files?'

'Two years ago, he was accused of the rape and murder of an under-age girl at Saint-Aubin. At the time he was working on a farm in the village. Arrested as a result of the public outcry, he was released a month later because there was no evidence against him. Since then, there has been no trace of him. In all likelihood he came to Paris.

We will make inquiries in the larger factories on the outskirts and I wouldn't be surprised that he too worked for Citroën. An inspector is already on his way there.'

'So that's one of the men who has been identified.'

'It's not much, but you will note that he is the key to the entire case. Colombani was good enough to let me have his file, which I have examined carefully. I have here a map he drew. It is very accurate. I also read in one of his memos that no Czech people were now living in the villages where the crimes were committed. But since there were a few Poles in the area some people spoke of a "Polish gang", thus throwing the blame for the massacre of the farmers on to them.'

'Where is all this leading?'

'When the group to which Carl belonged reached France, the men were sent to different places. He is the only one at that period who we have found to have been in the area located just south of Amiens. It was there that the three crimes were committed, all targeting rich, isolated farms and all involving elderly owners.'

'And the two farmers?'

'A little further to the east, near Saint-Quentin. I'm very confident that we'll find that Carl had either a woman or a friend somewhere thereabouts. He could get there by bike. Three years later, when the gang was formed . . .'

'Where do you think it was formed?'

'That I don't know, but as you'll see we shall find most of them on or around Quai de Javel. Victor Poliensky was still working for Citroën only weeks before the first attack took place.'

'You mentioned a leader.'

'Please let me complete my train of thought. Before the murder of Li'l Albert, or more accurately before his body was found in Place de la Concorde – if I differentiate between the two events you will soon see why – the gang was then on to its fourth slaughter and feeling completely safe. No one knew what any of them looked like. Our only witness was a little girl who had seen a woman torturing her mother. She had seen hardly anything of the men, who in any case had worn black cloths over their faces.'

'Did you find any of those black cloths in Rue du Roi-de-Sicile?'

'No. So the gang all felt safe. Who would have thought of looking for the Picardy murderers in a low dive in the ghetto? Isn't that right, Colombani?'

'Absolutely right.'

'Then suddenly Li'l Albert, feeling threatened by men who were following him around – as you will remember, when he phoned he said several times that they worked in relays – Li'l Albert, as I was saying, was knifed in the back in his own bar after calling on me to protect him. He had been intending to come to see me. That means he had information for me, and the others knew it. But here a question arises: why did they bother to move the body to Place de la Concorde?'

They looked at him in silence, each trying vainly to come up with an answer to this question, which Maigret had asked himself many times.

'I refer again to Colombani's file, which is remarkably detailed. For each of their raids on the farms, the gang

163

used different vehicles, preferably stolen vans. Nearly all of them were taken from streets around Place Clichy but all inside the eighteenth *arrondissement*. That is why inquiries were concentrated on that particular area. It was also in that part of Paris, though slightly further out of town, that the vehicles were recovered the day after the raids.'

'What do you conclude from that?'

'That the gang does not own a car. A vehicle has to be parked somewhere and can be traced.'

'Where does that leave the yellow car?'

'*The yellow car was not stolen.* If it had been we would know because the owner would have reported it, especially since it was almost brand-new.'

'I understand,' murmured the commissioner, while Monsieur Coméliau, who did not, scowled and looked annoyed.

'I should have thought of it sooner. I did consider the possibility at one point but dismissed the idea because it seemed too complicated and I always proceed on the basis that the truth is always simple. *The men who murdered Li'l Albert were not the men who dumped his body in Place de la Concorde.*'

'Who were they, then?'

'That I don't know, but we soon will.'

'How?'

'I have arranged for a personal ad to appear in the papers. Bear in mind that around five that afternoon, when he realized that we were unable to help him, Albert made a phone call, but not to us.'

'You think he was asking friends to rescue him?'

'Perhaps. But at least we do know that he arranged to meet somebody. And that somebody did not show up on time.'

'How do you know that?'

'You're forgetting that the yellow car broke down on Quai Henri-IV and the repair took some time to make.'

'So the two men it was bringing arrived too late?'

'Absolutely.'

'Hold on a moment! I'm looking at the file too. According to your fortune-teller, the car was parked outside the Petit Albert between about eight thirty and nine. But the body was not left on the pavement in Place de la Concorde until one in the morning.'

'Perhaps they came back, sir.'

'For the victim of a crime they had not committed so that they could dump him somewhere else?'

'Perhaps. I have no explanation. I'm merely stating that it's possible.'

'And what was happening meanwhile to Albert's wife?'

'Ah yes. Suppose they took her to a place of safety?'

'Why wouldn't they have killed her at the same time as they murdered her husband? She was probably as much in the know as him and in any case she had seen the murderers.'

'Who can say she hadn't gone out? When some kinds of men have certain kinds of business to transact, they prefer not having their wives around.'

'You don't think, detective chief inspector, that all of this is also keeping us away from the killers, who, as you pointed out, are currently at liberty in Paris?'

'What,' Maigret asked the examining magistrate, 'put us on to them in the first place, sir?'

'The body in Place de la Concorde, obviously.'

'Then why should it not do so again? You see, I believe that once we have understood, it shouldn't be hard to lay our hands on the whole gang. But first we have to understand.'

'So you think they killed the ex-waiter because he knew too much?'

'It's likely. I'm trying to discover how he knew what he knew. When I have the answer, I shall also know what he knew.'

The commissioner nodded approvingly and smiled. He could feel the antagonism between the two men. Meanwhile Colombani was also anxious to put in a word.

'Maybe the train . . . ?'

He knew the file inside out. Maigret made an encouraging gesture.

'What train are you talking about?' asked Coméliau.

'Since the most recent murders' – it was Colombani who replied and Maigret encouraged him with a look – 'we have had a small lead which we have deliberately not made public to avoid putting the gang on their guard. If you would look at the card numbered 5 which is attached to the file . . . The murders committed on 19 January took place in the home of the Rivals, unfortunately now deceased, as are their farm hand and maid. Their property is called Les Nonettes, probably because it was built on the ruins of an old nunnery. It is located some five kilometres from the village. There is a railway station in the village, Goderville, a halt for stopping trains. It's on the main Paris–Brussels line. I needn't point out that passengers coming from Paris are not frequent, because it would take hours to complete the journey by a train which stops at every small station. But on 19 January, at five in the afternoon, a man got out of the train with a return Paris–Goderville ticket.'

'Do we have a description of this man?'

'Sketchy. Youngish. Well dressed.'

The examining magistrate was also keen to make a discovery of his own:

'Did he have a foreign accent?'

'He didn't say anything. He passed through the village on the main road and was not seen again. On the other hand, the following morning at a few minutes past six, he took the train back to Paris from another out-of-the-way station, Moucher, twenty-one kilometres to the south. He did not use a taxi. He wasn't driven anywhere by any of the locals. It's hard to believe he would have spent the night tramping around just for the fun of it. His way must of necessity have taken him somewhere in the vicinity of Les Nonettes.'

Maigret had closed his eyes, overcome by a wave of exhaustion against which he fought with difficulty. He even fell half asleep standing up and he had let his pipe go out.

'When this information was passed to us,' continued Colombani, 'we went to the Compagnie du Nord and asked for the ticket. It's their practice for all tickets surrendered at stations to be kept for a certain period.'

'But you didn't recover it?'

'It wasn't handed in at Gare du Nord. This means that a traveller either got out on the wrong side on to the track or else that he lost himself in the crowd of passengers getting off at a suburban station and was able to make his way out without being seen, which is not difficult.'

'Is that what you were getting at, Maigret?'

'Yes, sir,' replied Maigret.

'And what conclusion do you draw from it?'

'I don't know. Li'l Albert could have been on the same train. Or maybe he just happened to have been at the station.'

He shook his head and went on:

'But I don't think so, otherwise they'd have started hounding him much sooner.'

'Which means?'

'Nothing. Yet he must have had some piece of tangible evidence in his possession, since the gang went to the trouble of searching his house from top to bottom after killing him. It's complicated. There's also the fact that Victor came back to the bar and snooped around.'

'So it's unlikely they found what they were looking for?'

'If they had, they'd hardly have sent the moron of the gang back to get it. No, I'd swear Victor went there on his own initiative, without the others knowing. If you want proof, there's the fact that they shot him in cold blood when they discovered that the police were on his tail and that he would lead us directly to them. Excuse me, gentlemen. My apologies, commissioner, I'm exhausted.'

He turned to Colombani.

'Shall I see you at five?'

'If you like.'

He seemed so limp, so weary, so irresolute that Monsieur Coméliau felt a twinge of guilt and murmured:

'Even so, you have produced some impressive results.'

And when Maigret had left the room:

'He's too old for sleepless nights. But why does he insist on doing everything himself?'

However he would have been very surprised if he had seen Maigret, just as he was about to step into a taxi, hesitate over the address and after a moment say:

'Quai de Charenton. I'll tell you where when we're there.'

Victor's visit to the Petit Albert bothered him. All the way there, he kept picturing him, tall, taking those catlike strides, with Lucas right behind him.

'What'll you have, sir?'

'Anything you like.'

Chevrier had entered fully into the spirit of his role. His wife must have been a good cook, for there were about twenty customers there.

'I'm going upstairs. Would you ask Irma to come up?'

She followed him up the stairs, wiping her hands on her apron. He looked all round the bedroom, which, with the windows wide opened, now smelled good and clean.

'Where did you put all the things that were lying around?'

He had made an inventory of them with Moers. But at that stage he had been looking for what the murderers had left behind. Now he was wondering about something else, something more specific: what had Victor personally come to retrieve?

'I pushed everything into the top drawer of the chest.'

Combs, a box containing hair pins, seashells inscribed with the name of a beach in Normandy, a free giveaway paper-knife, a broken propelling pencil, the usual oddments which clutter up houses.

'It's all here?'

'Even a half-opened packet of cigarettes and an old, broken pipe. Are we going to be here much longer?'

'I don't know. Are you getting tired of being here?'

'Me, no. But some of the customers get a bit too fresh, and my husband is beginning to get rattled. It won't be long before he punches somebody on the nose . . .'

He was still rummaging through the drawer and fished out a small German-made harmonica, which had seen a lot of use. To Irma's great surprise, he slipped it into his pocket.

'Is that all?' she asked.

'That's it.'

A few minutes later, from downstairs, he was phoning Monsieur Loiseau, who was taken aback by his question.

'Tell me: did Albert play the harmonica?'

'Not to my knowledge. He used to sing, but I never heard him play any instrument.'

Maigret remembered the harmonica which had been found in Rue du Roi-de-Sicile. The next moment he rang the number of the Lion d'Or.

'Listen, did Victor play the harmonica?'

'Sure he did. He even used to play it in the street as he walked along.'

'Was he the only one who played?'

'Serge Madok did too.'

'Did they both have their own harmonica?'

'I think so. Yes. I'm certain of it, because sometimes they used to play duets.'

But when Maigret had searched the room in the Lion d'Or, there had been only one harmonica.

What simple-minded Victor had come looking for in Quai de Charenton without telling the others, what ultimately he had died for, was his harmonica.

8.

What happened that afternoon would be added to the modest stock of anecdotes which a smiling Madame Maigret would relate at family gatherings.

That Maigret should have got home at two o'clock and gone to bed without having any lunch was not of itself all that unusual, although the first thing he always did whenever he got back to the apartment at any hour, night or day, was to go into the kitchen and lift the lids of the saucepans on the stove. He did say, however, that he had eaten already. But soon afterwards, while she probed a little deeper as he was getting undressed, he confessed that he had just helped himself to a slice of ham in the kitchen of the bar on Quai de Charenton.

She lowered the blinds, made sure her husband did not need for anything and glided silently out. Before the door had even closed he was in a deep sleep.

When she had done the washing-up and tidied the kitchen, she hesitated for some time before going back into their bedroom to fetch her knitting, which she had forgotten. First, she listened and, hearing regular breathing, turned the knob carefully and tiptoed back into the room without making any more sound than a nun in a cloister. It was at that point that, without ceasing to breathe like a man heavily asleep, he said in a thick voice:

'Can't believe it! Two and a half million in five months!'

His eyes were closed, and his face was flushed. She thought he was talking in his sleep but nevertheless stood stock-still so as not to wake him.

'Now where would you start if you wanted to spend that kind of money?'

She didn't dare reply, convinced that he was still dreaming. Then, still without moving his eyelids, he started to lose patience.

'Answer the question, Madame Maigret!'

'I have no idea,' she whispered. 'How much did you say?'

'Two and a half million. Probably a lot more. It's the minimum haul they took from the farms, and a sizeable part of it is in gold coins. Then there are the horses, obviously.'

He turned over heavily. One eye opened briefly and stared at his wife.

'The thing is, we can't get away from horse-racing.'

She knew he was not speaking for her benefit but for his own. She waited in the hope that he might go back to sleep so that she could withdraw the way she had come, without her knitting if necessary. He fell silent for some time, and she rather thought he had gone back to sleep.

'Listen, Madame Maigret. There's one small thing I want to know now. Where were there horse-races last Tuesday? Just in the Paris region, of course. Get on the phone now!'

'Who do you want me to phone?'

'Call the Pari-Mutuel. You'll find their number in the book.'

The phone was in the dining room, and the flex was too short for it to be brought into the bedroom. Madame Maigret still felt uneasy when she had to speak into the small metal disk, especially to someone she did not know.

'Shall I say I'm phoning on your behalf?'

'If you like.'

'What if they ask who I am?'

'They won't.'

By now both his eyes were open, and he was wide awake. She slipped into the next room and left the door open while she phoned. It did not take long. It was as if the person at the other end was used to answering such questions and obviously had the racing calendar at his fingertips, for he gave the information without hesitation. But when Madame Maigret went back into the bedroom to repeat to Maigret what she had been told, he was fast asleep, with his hands clenched tight and his breathing noisy enough for it to qualify as snoring.

She didn't like to wake him, decided that it was better to let him rest. But just in case, she left the communicating door ajar and from time to time looked at the clock with surprise, for her husband's afternoon naps rarely lasted very long.

At four o'clock she went into the kitchen to put the dinner on to cook. At half past, she glanced into the bedroom. Her husband was still sleeping. He looked as if he was dreaming that he was thinking: his eyebrows were knitted, his forehead was creased, and there was an odd curl to his lip.

But a little later, when she had sat down again in the

dining room, at her usual place by the window, she heard
a voice say impatiently:

'Well, what about this phone call?'

She scurried in and was surprised to see him sitting up
in bed.

'Is the number engaged?' he asked in a deadly serious
voice.

This produced a most singular effect on Madame Maigret. She felt almost frightened, as if her husband were
delirious.

'Oh, I got through all right. That was three hours ago.'

He stared at her in disbelief.

'What are you talking about? Look here, what time is it
now?'

'Quarter to five.'

He was not even aware that he had fallen asleep. He
thought he had closed his eyes for just as long as it took
to make a phone call.

'And where was it?'

'Vincennes.'

'What did I tell you?' he exulted.

He hadn't spoken to anyone, but he had thought about
it so much that it seemed that he had.

'Ring Rue des Saussaies . . . oo-90 . . . Ask to be put
through to Colombani's office . . .'

'What shall I tell him?'

'Nothing. I'll speak to him myself – that is if he's not
already on his way.'

Colombani was still at his desk. He was usually late for
meetings. He was very understanding and agreed to

meet Maigret in his apartment rather than at the Police Judiciaire.

She had, as he asked, made him a cup of strong coffee, but it had not been enough to wake him up completely. He had missed so much sleep that his eyelids were still pink and itched. His skin felt too tight. He hadn't had the energy to get dressed properly and had just put on his trousers, slippers and a dressing gown over his night shirt, the one with the collar which had small red crosses on it.

They made themselves comfortable in the dining room. They sat opposite each other with the decanter of calvados between them and, outside, on the white wall on the other side of the boulevard, in black letters, the names of Lhoste and Pépin.

They had known each other for long enough not to stand on ceremony. Colombani, who was short, like most Corsicans, wore lifts on his shoes, brightly coloured ties and a ring, with a real or maybe imitation diamond, on the third finger of his left hand. As a result, he was some-times thought to be one of the criminals he was looking for rather than the policeman hunting them.

'I've sent Janvier out to cover the race-courses,' said Maigret as he smoked his pipe. 'Where are they racing today?'

'Vincennes.'

'The same as last Tuesday, I'm wondering if it wasn't at Vincennes that Li'l Albert's adventures started. Prelimi-nary inquiries have already been made around the race-courses but without appreciable results. At that stage, we were only interested in an ex-waiter. Today, it's different. We now have to ask questions at the various betting windows, and especially those where the bigger bets are placed, five hundred or a thousand francs, and see if they have a customer, male, still young, with a foreign accent.'

'Maybe the course's own security people have already spotted him?'

'Well, I don't suppose he goes by himself. Two and a half million in five months takes some spending.'

'And it must come to a lot more than that,' said Colombani. 'In my report, I only gave figures I was sure of. They are the amounts the gang definitely got away with. But it's very likely the farmers had other hiding places whose locations were extracted by torture. I wouldn't be surprised if the real total was four millions and upwards. What could those lousy scum from Rue du Roi-de-Sicile have spent it on? Not on clothes. They never went out. They ate and drank at home. Even allowing for the fact that there are five of them, it would take a good long time for them to eat and drink their way through even one million francs' worth. And yet their raids had followed at short intervals.'

'The leader must have taken the lion's share.'

'I'm wondering why the others would have allowed him to do that.'

There were a lot more questions which Maigret kept asking himself, so many in fact that there were times when he got sick of thinking and, passing one hand across his forehead, he would fix his eyes on an arbitrary point, the geranium in the distant window, for instance. But it was no good. Even here, in his own home, he was completely bogged down in this investigation and felt anxious about everything that was going on at that same moment in Paris and the suburbs. He had not yet arranged for Maria to be transferred to the infirmary in the Santé prison. But he had made sure that the afternoon editions of the papers published the name of the hospital to which she had been taken.

'I assume you've sent a few inspectors out there to stand guard?' asked Colombani.

'Four, in addition to the uniformed men. The hospital has several exits. Today is visiting day.'

'Do you think they'll make a move?'

'I don't know. But given that they're all crazy about her, I wouldn't be surprised if at least one of them would try something regardless of the risks. Not to mention the fact that every one of them probably believes that he's the father. And if they believe that, they'll want to see the kid and the mother. It's a dangerous game, and the danger comes not so much from me but from the others.'

'I don't get you.'

'They killed Victor Poliensky, didn't they? Why? Because it was very likely he'd lead us to them. If any one of them looks as if he's about to fall into our hands, I'd be amazed if the others would let him go on living.'

Maigret drew on his pipe, looking pensive. Colombani lit a gold-tipped cigarette and said:

'The first thing they'll try to do is contact their leader, especially if their funds are running low.'

Maigret looked at him mildly but then his eyes hardened. He got to his feet, thumped the table with one hand and cried:

'Oaf! What a fool I am! That never occurred to me!'

'But you don't know where he lives . . .'

'That's just the point! I'd bet they don't know either. The man who set up the whole operation and gives the villains their orders is certain to have covered his back. What was it the hotel-keeper told me? That *he would come to Rue du Roi-de-Sicile and give them instructions before they went out on every job?* Got it? Has the penny started to drop?'

'Not quite.'

'What do we know about him, or what can we deduce? We're looking for him at race meetings. Do you think they are more stupid than us? You're quite right! Even as we speak they are unquestionably trying to track him down. To ask him for money, perhaps, but in any case to bring him up to date and ask for his advice or for new instructions. I bet none of them slept in a bed last night. Where would you expect them to go?'

'To Vincennes?'

'It's more than likely. If they haven't split up, they'll have sent at least one of their number. But if they have separated without agreeing what each should do, it wouldn't surprise me if all three of them have gone there. We had a glorious opportunity to round up the lot of them without even knowing who they are! It's easy to spot men of that type in a crowd. And to think that Janvier is there, and I haven't told him how to act accordingly! If we had thirty inspectors in the paddock and public enclosures we'd collar the lot of them! What's the time now?'

'It's too late! The sixth race finished half an hour ago.'

'Dammit! You think you've covered everything! When I went to bed at two, I was convinced that I had done all I could do. I had men studying payslips from Citroën and searching the Javel district. Laennec Hospital is surrounded. Every part of Paris where men like the Czechs might go to ground is being combed. Down-and-outs and tramps are being formally questioned. Hotels are being checked. Moers, in his lab on the top floor, is analysing every last hair we found in the rooms in Rue du Roi-de-Sicile.

'Meanwhile, our gallant band have probably had an opportunity to exchange a few words with their boss.'

It seemed that Colombani was also a keen race-goer, for he wasn't far wrong. The phone rang. It was Janvier.

'I'm still at Vincennes, sir. I tried to get you at HQ.'

'Is the last race over?'

'Finished half an hour ago. I've stayed on with the cashiers who man the betting windows. It was hard trying to get anything out of them while the racing was going on, because they work under such pressure. It beats me how they don't make mistakes. I questioned them about the bets, as you'll remember. A man who sits at a thousand-franc window was immediately struck by my question. He's travelled around central Europe and is able to tell different languages from each other. "A Czech?" he said. "I've got one who persistently bets the limit, almost always puts it on outsiders. For a while, I thought he must be from the embassy."'

'Why?'

'Seems he's a well-set-up sort, well bred, always elegantly turned out. He loses most of the time but doesn't seem to mind. He just gives a little smile. But that's not the reason why the cashier remembers him, it's the woman who regularly accompanies him.'

Maigret gave a sigh of relief and turned to Colombani with a delighted glance as if to say:

'We've got them!'

'A woman! At last!' he cried into the mouthpiece. 'Is she foreign?'

'A Parisienne. Hang on! That's precisely why I'm still at the race-course. If I'd been able to talk to the cashier sooner, he would have pointed both of them out to me, for they were here this afternoon.'

'What about the woman?'

'Well, she's very young, very good-looking, it seems, wears the very best haute couture clothes. But that's not all, sir. The cashier told me that she's a movie actress. He doesn't go to the cinema very often and doesn't know the names of the stars. But he reckons she probably isn't a star, but takes the supporting roles. I mentioned a whole list of names but got no reaction.'

'What time is it?'

'Quarter to six.'

'Since you're out at Vincennes, I want you to go to Joinville. It's not far. Ask your cashier to go with you.'

'He says he'll do whatever he can to help.'

'There are studios just after the bridge. Generally film-producers keep photographs of actors, including those who play small parts, and they use their collection when they are casting a new film. Got that?'

'Got it. Where should I call you?'

'At home.'

He was relaxed when he sat down in his chair again.

'It might work,' he said. 'Provided he's our Czech, obviously.'

He filled the gold-rimmed liqueur glasses, knocked his pipe out and refilled it.

'I have a feeling we're going to have a busy night. Did you arrange for that little girl to be brought?'

'She's been on the way since three o'clock. I'll be going soon to meet her at Gare du Nord myself.'

The little girl from the Manceau farm, miraculously the sole survivor of the carnage and the only one who saw any of the assailants: Maria, now lying on her hospital bed with a baby by her side.

The phone rang again. From now on, he would never know what to expect when he picked up the receiver.

'Hello?'

Again, Maigret's eyes remained fixed on his colleague, but this time they were filled with irritation. He spoke in a muffled voice. For some time, he merely muttered answers at almost regular intervals.

'Yes . . . Yes . . . Yes . . .'

Colombani tried to work out what was going on. But not being able to understand was made all the more galling by the fact that he could hear a buzzing sound from the receiver punctuated at intervals by stray, detached syllables.

'In ten minutes? . . . Of course . . . Exactly as I promised . . .'

Why did Maigret seem as if he were holding back?
Again, his mood had changed completely. No child waiting
for Christmas was ever more impatient or excited, yet he
was forcing himself to be calm and even to look grim-
faced.

When he hung up, instead of saying anything to Colombani, he opened the door which led to the kitchen.

'Your aunt and her husband are on their way,' he said.

'Eh? . . . What are you talking about? . . . But . . .'

He winked repeatedly at her but it did no good.

'I know. I was surprised too. It must be something serious, something unexpected that's cropped up. She says she
wants to talk to us right away.'

He put his head round the door so that he could fire off
more faces at his wife. She had no idea what to make of
this.

'Well, really! This is a surprise and no mistake. As long
as nothing serious has happened . . .'

'Unless it's something to do with the inheritance?'

'What inheritance?'

'Her uncle's.'

When he returned to his visitor, Colombani had a knowing smile on his face.

'Look, I'm sorry, old son. My wife's aunt will be here in
a moment. I've just got time to get dressed. I'm not kicking you out but I hope you understand . . .'

The detective chief inspector of the Sûreté swallowed
the contents of his glass, stood up and wiped his mouth.

'Don't worry about it. I know what it's like. Will you give me a ring if you hear anything?'

'I promise.'

'I have a feeling you'll be phoning me quite soon. I'm even wondering if it's worth me going back to Rue des Saussaies. No, I won't! If you don't object, I think I'll wander over to Quai des Orfèvres.'

'That's fine! I'll see you later.'

Maigret almost pushed him out on to the landing. Then, the moment the door was closed, he hurried across the room and looked out of the window. To his left, further along the road than Lhoste & Pépin, there was the shop of a wine and coal merchant who hailed from Auvergne. It was painted yellow. He fixed his eyes on its door, beside which stood a green plant.

'That was all a trick, wasn't it?' asked Madame Maigret.

'Of course! I didn't want Colombani to meet the people who will be coming up the stairs at any moment.'

As he spoke, he happened to lay one hand on the window-ledge, just where Colombani had been standing a few moments earlier. It landed on paper, a newspaper. He glanced down at it and saw that it was folded open at the page carrying the personal small ads: one had been ringed in blue.

'Of all the . . .' he muttered through gritted teeth.

Now there is a long-standing rivalry between the nation-wide Sûreté and Paris's Police Judiciaire, and joy is unconfined when someone from Rue des Saussaies pulls a fast one on a colleague from Quai des Orfèvres.

Actually, Colombani had not taken a particularly savage

revenge on Maigret for lying about the aunt. He had merely left behind a clear signal that he had understood.

The advertisement which had appeared in every newspaper that morning and also at midday in the racing papers, said, with the usual abbreviations:

Friends of Albert, indispensable for security contact Maigret urgent home address 132, Boulevard Richard-Lenoir. Absolute discretion guaranteed.

It was them, they had just phoned from the Auvergnat's shop across the way to make sure that the advert was not a hoax or a trap, and to hear Maigret repeat his guarantee and lastly to make sure the coast was clear.

'I need you to go out and walk around for a while, Madame Maigret. Don't hurry back. Wear your hat with the green feather.'

'Why my hat with the green feather?'

'Because soon it will be spring.'

Maigret watched them from his window as they crossed the road, looking like two men on an important mission. But from this distance he was only able to recognize one of them.

A few moments earlier, he had known absolutely nothing about the men who were on their way to see him, or about their background. He would only have bet that they too were followers of the turf.

'Colombani is hanging around somewhere, watching them,' he muttered.

And once Colombani got the scent he was quite capable of blowing his cover. It was just the kind of sly practical joke that colleagues regularly played on each other.

Especially as Colombani probably knew Jo the Boxer better than he did.

He was short, thick-set, with a broken nose and scarred eyelids over light-blue eyes. He invariably wore dog-tooth-checked suits and loud ties. In the aperitif hour he was always to be found in one of the small bars on Avenue de Wagram. He had been hauled up before Maigret in his office at least a dozen times, always for different misdemeanours, and each time he had managed to get away with it.

Was he really dangerous? He would have liked people to think so, for he deliberately cultivated his image as a 'bruiser'. It was his affectation to look as if he were part of the criminal fraternity, but members of the criminal fraternity did not trust him and even regarded him with a certain contempt.

Maigret opened the door for them and put out fresh glasses on the table. They entered looking awkward and remained suspicious despite the reassurances. Their eyes darted into every corner, and they were visibly nervous about the closed doors.

'Nothing to be scared of here. There is no hidden stenographer, no dictaphones. Look here, this is my bedroom.'

He showed them the unmade bed.

'This is the bathroom, that's the clothes cupboard, and here you have the kitchen, which Madame Maigret has just vacated in your honour.'

The simmering soup smelled good, and an uncooked chicken already barded with strips of fat bacon sat on the table.

'This door? It's the last one, the spare bedroom we keep for friends. It hasn't been aired. It smells musty for the very good reason that our friends never sleep here. It's only used by my sister-in-law on two or three nights a year.

'And now, to work!'

He held out his drink to clink glasses with them. As he did so, he looked questioningly at the man who was with Jo.

'This is Ferdinand,' said the boxer.

Maigret racked his brains but came up with nothing. The man was tall and thin, and his face with the huge nose and small, quick mouse eyes did not remind him of anyone or of any name.

'He runs a garage not far from Porte de Maillot. Just a small one, of course.'

It was odd to see the both of them standing there, unsure about whether they should sit, not because they felt intimidated, but as a precaution. Men like these never like to be too far from a door.

'You seemed to be saying there's some sort of danger.'

'Actually two sorts of danger. First, that the Czechs will spot you, in which case I wouldn't give much for your chances of survival.'

Jo and Ferdinand eyed each other with surprise. They thought there must be some mistake.

'What Czechs?'

There had been no mention of any Czechs in the papers.

'The Picardy gang.'

This time, they understood and suddenly became more serious.

'We never got on the wrong side of them.'

'Maybe. But we'll talk about that later. It would be so much better to chat if you were sitting down nice and cosy.'

With his tough-man swagger, Jo settled into an armchair, but Ferdinand, who did not know Maigret, sat on the edge of his straight-backed seat.

'The second danger . . .' said Maigret, observing them while he lit his pipe. 'Haven't you noticed anything today?'

'The place is swarming with cops . . . Oh sorry! . . .'

'No offence taken. Not only is the place swarming with cops, as you say, but most of them are on the hunt, looking for a certain number of people, and in particular a couple of men who own a yellow car.'

Ferdinand smiled.

'I don't think for one moment,' said Maigret, 'that it'll still be yellow and have the same number plate. But let's leave that for now. If Police Judiciaire inspectors had got to you first, I might have been able to get you off the hook. But did you see the man who just left?'

Jo muttered: 'Colombani.'

'Did he spot you?'

'We waited until he was safely on the bus.'

'It means that Rue des Saussaies is also on the hunt. Fall into their hands and you wouldn't have avoided coming up against Coméliau.'

It was a name to conjure with, for both men knew, at least at second hand, the examining magistrate's reputation for severity.

'Whereas, by coming to see me, all friendly, as you have done, we can have a nice little chat.'

'We know next to nothing.'

'What you do know will be enough. You were friends of Albert?'

'He was a decent sort.'

'A joker, right?'

'We met him at the races.'

'I thought so.'

That put both men in their context. Ferdinand's garage was probably not open to the public very often. Perhaps he didn't sell stolen vehicles, because it takes a sophisticated organization plus a lot of specialized equipment to dress them up. Moreover, these two were the sort who don't much like getting their hands dirty. It was more likely that Ferdinand bought up old cars cheap, which he did up just enough to make them attractive to the easily duped.

In bars, on race-courses, in hotel lobbies, it's easy to meet gullible individuals who are always only too delighted to snap up an amazing bargain. Sometimes the deal is clinched by a confidential whisper to the effect that the car had been stolen from a star of the silver screen.

'Were the two of you at Vincennes last Tuesday?'

They had to look at each other again, not this time to align their stories, but to help them to remember.

'Wait a sec. Listen, Ferdinand, wasn't it last Tuesday you backed a winner, Semiramis?'

'Yes.'

'Then we were there.'

'What about Albert?'

'Ah, now I remember! That was the day there was a downpour during the third race. Albert was there. I saw him in the distance.'

'You didn't speak to him?'

'No, because he wasn't in the public enclosures but in the paddock. The both of us always stick to the public areas. He does too, normally, but that Tuesday he had his wife with him. It was their wedding anniversary or similar. He'd told me about it a few days before. He was even thinking about buying a cheapish car, and Ferdinand had said he'd look out for something for him, genuine, a nice little runner.'

'After that?'

'After what?'

'What happened the next day?'

They again exchanged uncertain looks, and Maigret had to put them back on the right track once more.

'He phoned you at the garage on Wednesday at about five o'clock, didn't he?'

'No, at the Pélican, in Avenue de Wagram. We're nearly always there at that time of day.'

'Now, I want to know what he said exactly, word for word if possible. Which of you answered?'

'Me,' said Jo.

'Think. Take your time.'

'He seemed in a mighty hurry. Sounded flustered.'

'I know . . .'

'To begin with, I didn't understand what it was all about.

He jumbled everything up because he was going so fast, as if he was afraid we'd be cut off.'

'I also know that. He phoned me four or five times that day . . .'

'Oh.'

Jo and Ferdinand gave up trying to understand.

'So if he rang you, you must know . . .' said Jo.

'Carry on anyway.'

'He said there were these three men following him and that he was scared, but he said he might have found a way of shaking them off.'

'Did he say what this way was?'

'No, but he seemed happy enough with his idea.'

'Then?'

'He said, more or less: "It's a really terrible business, but we might be able to make something of it." Don't forget, that you promised . . .'

'I repeat my promise,' said Maigret. 'The pair of you will walk out of here as free as when you came in, and you won't be bothered afterwards, whatever you tell me – provided, that is, you tell me everything.'

'So you knew him as well as we did?'

'More or less.'

'Right! Never mind! Then Albert said: "Call round and see me tonight at eight. We'll talk it over."'

'What did you think he meant by that?'

'Wait a minute, he also had time to say something else before hanging up: "I'll pack Nine off to the cinema." Do you see? That meant that there was something serious in the wind . . .'

'One moment. Had Albert ever worked with the both of you before?'

'Never. What would he have done? You know what line of work we're in. It's not nine-to-five stuff. Albert was a steady sort, led a regular life.'

'But that didn't stop him thinking that he might make a bit out of what he had discovered.'

'Maybe it didn't, I don't know. Wait. I'm trying to remember how he put it, but it's gone. He mentioned the gang from the north.'

'So you decided you'd meet him as arranged.'

'Did we have any choice?'

'Listen, Jo, stop playing the fool! For once there's nothing riding on this for you, so you can be frank with me. You thought your pal Albert had got the goods on the Picardy gang. You knew, because you read it in the paper, that they'd got away with millions, and you were wondering if there wasn't some way of getting your hands on a slice of it. Is that it?'

'That's what I thought Albert meant, yes.'

'Good. We're agreed on that. Next?'

'We both went.'

'And your car broke down on Quai Henri-IV, which leads me to think that the yellow Citroën wasn't quite as brand new as it looked.'

'We'd done it up to sell it. We hadn't been banking on using it ourselves.'

'So you reached Quai de Charenton a good half an hour late. The shutters were closed. You opened the door, which was not locked.'

They looked at each other again, gloomily.

'And you found your pal Albert, who had been killed with a knife.'

'That's the size of it.'

'What did you do?'

'At first we thought he hadn't croaked because the body was still warm.'

'What next?'

'We saw that the house had been searched. We remembered that Nine would soon be back from the pictures. There's a cinema not far from there, in Charenton, just by the canal. So we went there.'

'What were you thinking of doing?'

'We didn't know, really, I swear. We weren't looking forward to it, either of us. To start with it's no fun having to break news like that to a woman. And then we started wondering if anyone in the gang had spotted us. Ferdinand and me talked it over.'

'And you decided to pack Nine off to the country?'

'Yes.'

'Is she very far away?'

'She's out down Corbeil way, staying at an inn by the Seine where we go fishing now and then. Ferdinand's got a boat there.'

'Didn't she want to see Albert?'

'We talked her out of it. When we drove along the river-bank again, later that night, there wasn't anybody around the house. You could still see light under the door, because we never thought to switch it off.'

'Why did you move the body?'

'That was Ferdinand's idea.'

Maigret turned to Jo's companion, who looked at the floor.

'Why?' repeated Maigret.

'I can't explain. I was in a state. When we were at the inn, we'd had a few drinks, to steady the nerves. I kept telling myself the neighbours must have seen the car and might even have had a good look at us. Also if it got out that it was Albert who was dead, they'd come looking for Nine, who wouldn't be able to keep her mouth shut.'

'So you laid a false trail.'

'You could say that. The police aren't as interested in following up on run-of-the-mill cases, when the crime seems straightforward, such as when, for example, a man is stabbed to death for his money . . .'

'And was it also you who had the idea of making a slit in his raincoat?'

'We had to, if we were going to make it look like he'd been killed on the streets.'

'And also to rearrange his face for him?'

'There was no choice. He couldn't feel anything. That way we thought the case would be closed quickly, and we'd be kept out of it.'

'Is that all?'

'That's everything, I swear. Isn't that right, Jo? The next day I resprayed the car, and changed the number plate.'

It was evident they were now getting ready to leave.

'Just a minute. Have you been sent anything since?'

'Sent what?'

'An envelope, with something in it.'

'No.'

It was plain to see that they were telling the truth. They had been genuinely surprised by the question.

And, as Maigret asked it, he saw a possible solution to the problem which had been bothering him most for the last few days. It had been supplied by Ferdinand unwittingly, only minutes before. Hadn't Albert told him over the phone that he had just found a way of getting the gang that was following him off his back?

Hadn't he asked for an envelope at the last brasserie he had been seen in, just after he had phoned his friends?

He had in his possession, in his pocket, something which implicated the Czechs. One of them had always kept him in full view. Wasn't being seen to drop an envelope in a letterbox a good way of getting whoever was following him off his back?

Slipping the document into the envelope was merely a diversion.

But whose address had he written on it?

He picked up the phone and called the Police Judiciaire.

'Hello? Who's that? . . . Bodin? . . . A job for you, and it's urgent . . . How many inspectors are on the premises now . . . Eh? Just four? One must stay on duty there, of course. Take the other three. Share out all the post offices in Paris between you . . . wait! . . . including the one at Charenton, where I want you to begin yourself. Question the staff at the poste restante counter. Somewhere there's got to be a letter addressed to Albert Rochain which has been waiting to be collected for a few days . . . Yes, get it and bring it to me . . . No, not to my home. I'll be in the office in half an hour.'

He looked at the two men and smiled.

'Fancy another?'

They clearly weren't keen on calvados but accepted out of politeness.

'Can we go now?'

They still didn't trust him completely and stood up like schoolboys when the teacher lets the class out for break.

'We're not going to be dragged in any deeper?'

'We won't need to involve you any further. All I ask is that you don't warn Nine.'

'She won't be bothered either?'

'Why should she be?'

'Go easy on her, will you? If you knew how much she loved her Albert!'

When the door closed behind them, Maigret turned off the gas. The soup was starting to boil over and spill on to the stove.

He was pretty sure that his two bravos had lied to some extent. According to Dr Paul, they hadn't waited to smuggle Nine to a place of safety before battering their friend's face to a pulp.

But that did not change things much and in the last analysis they had proved to be sufficiently cooperative for Maigret to not want to make life hard for them. Deep down, people like them can feel shame. Just like everybody else.

9.

The office was blue with smoke. Colombani was sitting in a corner with his legs stretched out in front of him. A few moments earlier, the commissioner of the Police Judiciaire had also been there. Inspectors came and went. Coméliau, the examining magistrate, had just phoned.

Again, Maigret picked up the phone.

'Hello? . . . Marchand? . . . Maigret here . . . Yes, the real one . . . What do you mean? You've got another friend called Maigret? . . . A count, eh? . . . No: no relation . . .'

It was seven o'clock. The man at the other end of the line was the general manager of the Folies-Bergère.

'What do you want now?' said Marchand in his throaty voice. 'God knows it's not a good time for me. I've just got a few minutes to dash out and grab a quick snack before the doors open. Unless you fancy a bite to eat with me? What would you say to the Chope Montmartre, for example? . . . Ten minutes? . . . See you there.'

Janvier was in the office looking very pleased with himself. It was he who had just brought a handsome, enlarged photograph from Joinville, like the ones which, personally autographed, are found hanging in actors' dressing rooms. This one was also signed, in a spiky, ultra-confident hand: Francine Latour.

The woman was pretty, still very young. Her address appeared on the back: 121, Rue de Longchamp, at Passy.

'Apparently she is currently appearing in the Folies-Bergère,' Janvier had said.

'Did the Pari-Mutuel man recognize her?'

'Formally identified her. I'd have brought him back with me, but he was already late and lives in fear of his wife. But if we need him we can call him at home at any time. He lives not far from here, on Ile Saint-Louis, and he has a telephone.'

Francine Latour also had a telephone. Maigret called her apartment, planning to say nothing and hang up immediately if anyone answered. But, as he had suspected, she was not there.

'Feel like going over there, Janvier? Take someone discreet with you. I don't want to attract any attention.'

'Want us to have a quiet look round the apartment?'

'Not straight away. Wait for my call. One of you had better stay in a bar close by. Tell him to phone in and leave us the number.'

He frowned, making sure he remembered everything. The officer sent out to Citroën's offices had at least come back with one piece of information: Serge Madok had worked there for two years.

Maigret walked into the inspectors' office.

'All right, listen now. I'm probably going to need a lot of people this evening or tonight. It would be best if you all stayed here on the job. Take turns to go out and get something to eat locally, or else send out for sandwiches and beers. I'll see you later. Coming, Colombani?'

'I thought you were having dinner with Marchand?'

'You know him too, don't you?'

Marchand, who had begun as a tout reselling pass-out tickets outside theatres, was one of the leading Paris personalities. He had not lost his rough manner or vulgar way of speaking. He was in the restaurant, elbows on the table, holding a vast menu. When the two policemen came in, he said to the head waiter:

'Something light, Georges . . . Let's see . . . Got any partridges?'

'With cabbage, Monsieur Marchand.'

'Sit yourself down, old son. Ah! I see we've got the Sûreté in tonight. Bring another plate, Georges. What do you two say to *perdrix au chou*, eh? Hang on! And also to start, how about *truites au bleu*. Are the trout live, Georges?'

'You can see them in the display tank, Monsieur Marchand.'

'A few hors d'oeuvres while we wait. That's it. And a soufflé to finish with if you want.'

It was his passion. Even when eating alone he would order meals like this at lunch or dinner. And that is what he called 'eating light', a snack. Maybe, after the show, he would settle down to a proper supper?

'Well now. And what can I do you for? Not found anything fishy in my box of delights, I hope?'

It was too soon for serious talking. It was now the wine waiter's turn to approach. Marchand took a good few minutes choosing the wines.

'Right, I'm all ears.'

'If I tell you something, will you keep it to yourself?'

'Listen, you're forgetting that I probably know more secrets than any other man in Paris. Look, I hold the fate of hundreds, make that thousands, of married couples in my hands. Keep my trap shut? It's what I do all day!'

He was a real card. The fact was that he never stopped talking from morning to night, but it was perfectly true that he never said what he really meant.

'Do you know Francine Latour?'

'She's appearing in a couple of comic sketches with Dréan.'

'What do you think of her?'

'What do I think of her? She's a decent piece of skirt. Come back and ask me again in ten years.'

'Does she have talent?'

Marchand gave Maigret a look of comic surprise.

'Why are you asking if she's got talent? I don't know exactly how old she is but she can't be more than twenty and she's already getting her clothes from the top dress-makers. I even think she's started having diamonds. I know for a fact that last week she turned up wearing a mink coat. What else do you want to know?'

'Does she have lovers?'

'She's got one. Everybody's got one.'

'Know who he is?'

'I don't see how I could help not knowing him.'

'A foreigner, isn't he?'

'Nowadays they're nearly all foreigners. It's as if all France is good for any more is supplying faithful husbands.'

'Listen, Marchand. This is a lot more serious than you might think.'

'When are you going to get the cuffs on him?'

'Tonight, I hope. It's not what you imagine.'

'At all events, he's used to it. If I remember right, he's been up in court twice for passing dud cheques or similar. At the minute he seems flush.'

'What's his name?'

'Backstage they all call him Monsieur Jean. His real name is Bronsky. He's a Czech.'

'A dud cheque,' added Colombani. Maigret shrugged his shoulders.

'He dabbled for a while in the film business. I think he's still got a finger in that pie,' continued Marchand, who was quite capable of reeling off the CVs of all Paris' celebrities, including the most unsavoury customers. 'Good-looking, likeable, generous. Women adore him, and men are wary of his charm.'

'Is he in love with her?'

'I'd say so. But whether he is or not, he hardly ever lets the girl out of his sight. They reckon he's jealous.'

'Where do you think the both of them are right now?'

'If there were any horse-races this afternoon, it's very likely he went with her. A woman who's been buying her clothes in Rue de la Paix for the last five or six months and wears a new mink coat doesn't get easily bored at race-courses. Just now, they'll be having a pre-dinner drink in a bar on the Champs-Élysées. She's not due on stage until half past nine. She usually gets to the theatre at around nine. So they have plenty of time to have dinner at Fouquet's or Maxim's or Ciro's. If you want to find them . . .'

'Not now. Does Bronsky go to the theatre with her?'

'Almost always. He sees her to her dressing room, hangs around backstage for a while, then makes straight for the bar just off the main lobby and passes the time of day with Félix. After the second sketch he joins her in her dressing room and as soon as she's ready he goes off with her. It's pretty rare if they don't go on to a cocktail party somewhere.'

'Does he live with her?'

'Very likely. But that's something you'd best ask her concierge.'

'Have you seen him these last few days?'

'I saw him just yesterday.'

'And did he seem more on edge than usual?'

'Men like him are always a bit on edge, you know. When you're walking a tightrope . . . Listen, I'll say this: as I see it, the rope is about to break. It's a great shame for the kid! Still, now she's got herself a decent wardrobe, the rest will take care of itself. She'll have every chance of finding someone much better for herself . . .'

As he talked, Marchand ate, drank, wiped his mouth with his serviette, waved familiarly to people who came in or were leaving and still managed to find a moment to summon the head waiter or ask for the wine list.

'Do you know how he got started?'

Marchand, who was constantly reminded of his own origins by the small-circulation scandal sheets, answered somewhat tersely:

'Now that, old son, is a question you don't ask a gentleman.'

But within moments he was ready to resume where he had left off.

'What I do know is that for a time he ran an agency for extras.'

'Was that a long time ago?'

'A couple of months. I could find out.'

'There's no point. In fact, I'd rather you didn't mention anything about this discussion to anybody, especially tonight.'

'Will you be coming to the theatre?'

'No.'

'I prefer it that way. I would have asked you not to pursue your inquiries on my premises.'

'I don't want to run any risks, Marchand. My picture and Colombani's have appeared in the papers too often. According to what you say about him and what I know of him, this man is clever enough to spot any of my inspectors.'

'Seems to me, my friend, that you're taking this business very seriously, aren't you? Help yourself to more partridge.'

'There's going to be big trouble.'

'I see.'

'There's been trouble already. A lot of it.'

'Ah! Well, don't tell me anything. I'd rather read all about it in the papers tomorrow or the day after. It could put me in a spot if he asks me to have a drink with him tonight. Come on, eat up! What do you think of this Châteauneuf? They've only got fifty bottles of it left, and I've told them to put them aside for me. Now there are just forty-nine. Shall I ask for another?'

'Better not. We'll be working all night.'

They went their different ways a quarter of an hour

later, feeling somewhat sluggish after such a large meal liberally washed down with too much wine.

'Let's hope he keeps his mouth shut,' said Colombani.

'He will.'

'By the way, Maigret, did your aunt come up with any useful leads?'

'She did indeed. I now know virtually everything about Li'l Albert.'

'I thought you might. There's nothing like women for being well informed. Especially aunts who are just up from the country. Want to tell me?'

They had a little time to kill. Any easing of the tension was welcome ahead of a night which promised to be eventful. They chatted as they walked back along the pavements.

'You were right earlier. We would most probably have rounded them all up at Vincennes. Now, provided Jean Bronsky doesn't suspect that we're closing in on him . . .'

'We'll do everything we can, won't we?'

They reached the Police Judiciaire building at around nine thirty. There was important news. An inspector was waiting for them. He said excitedly:

'Sir, Carl Lipschitz is dead! It happened virtually before my very eyes! I was standing in the shadows in Rue de Seine, a hundred metres from the hospital. For some time, I'd been hearing noises to my right. There was someone there, in the darkness, who seemed reluctant to step forwards. Then I heard the sound of running footsteps, and a shot was fired. It was so close that my first thought was that someone was shooting at me, and I automatically got out my revolver. I sensed rather than saw a falling body and the outline of someone running off. I opened fire.'

'Did you kill him?'

'I aimed for his legs and was lucky. I got him with my second shot. This man, the one who was running away, also fell to the ground.'

'Who was it?'

'The kid. The one they call Pietr. We didn't have far to carry him because the hospital was on the other side of the street.'

'So Pietr shot at Carl?'

'Yes.'

'Were they together?'

'No, I don't think so. I believe Pietr was following Carl and shot him.'

'What is he saying?'

'The kid? Nothing. He has kept his mouth shut. His eyes are bright and feverish. He seemed happy or dead pleased with himself to be in the hospital and as he passed through the corridors he kept looking eagerly all round him.'

'Because of Maria, of course! She's still there! Is he seriously hurt?'

'The bullet got him in the left knee. They'll be operating on him now, as we speak.'

'What about his pockets?'

On Maigret's desk were two small collections of objects which had been carefully laid out.

'The first one is the contents of Carl's pockets. The other one is what was in Pietr's.'

'Is Moers upstairs?'

'He rang down to let us know that he'll be in his lab all night.'

'Ask him to come here. And I want someone to go up to Records. I need the card and the whole file on a man named Jean Bronsky. I haven't got any prints for him, but he's been up in court twice and was probably given an eighteen-month jail sentence.'

He also sent men out to Rue de Provence, opposite the Folies-Bergère, with strict instructions to keep out of sight at all times. He told them:

'Before you go wait until you see a photo of Bronsky. Only if he attempts to get on a train or a plane is he to be apprehended. But I don't think that will happen.'

Carl Lipschitz's wallet contained forty-two thousand-franc notes, an identity card made out in his name and a second card in an Italian name: Filipino. He didn't smoke, for he wasn't carrying cigarettes, a pipe or a lighter, but he had a pocket torch, two handkerchiefs, one filthy, a cinema ticket bearing that day's date, a penknife and an automatic revolver.

'You see?' Maigret remarked to Colombani. 'And there we were, imagining that we had thought of everything.'

He pointed to the cinema ticket.

'They had the same thought. Buying a cinema ticket is better than wandering around the streets. You can spend hours in the dark. You can even get some sleep in one of the boulevard cinemas that stay open all night.'

In Pietr's pockets there were just thirty-eight francs in coins. A wallet contained two photographs, one of Maria, a small passport photo which must have been taken the previous year when she had done her hair differently, and a picture of two country people, a man and a woman, sitting by their front door, in central Europe, insofar as could be judged by the style of the house.

No identity papers. Cigarettes, a lighter, a pocket notebook, of which a number of pages were covered by fine handwriting in pencil.

'Looks like poetry.'

'Actually, I'd say that's exactly what it is.'

Moers was over the moon to have the two sets of objects which he could rush off with to his lair under the eaves. Soon after this, an inspector deposited Bronsky's file on the desk. The photo, hard and cruel as anthropometric photographs always are, did not match exactly the description Marchand had given for this man, who was still young, looked drawn and had a two-day beard and a prominent Adam's apple.

'Has Janvier phoned?'

'He said everything was quiet and that you can reach him on Passy 62-41.'

'Get me the number.'

He began to read half aloud. According to his file, Bronsky had been born in Prague and was now thirty-five years old. He had studied at the University of Vienna, after which he lived in Berlin for two years. There he married a Hilda Braun but when he entered France at the age of twenty-eight he was alone. His papers were in order. He was already giving his profession as 'film director', and his first address was a hotel on Boulevard Raspail.

'Janvier on the phone, sir.'

'Is that you, young man? Have you eaten? . . . Listen carefully. I'm going to send you a car with two men.'

'There are two of us here already,' protested Janvier in an aggrieved voice.

'Never mind that now. Listen to what I say. When they get there, leave them outside. They mustn't show themselves. It is vital that anyone going into the building or getting out of a taxi should not suspect that they are there. I want you and your colleague to go inside. Wait until the lights have been turned off in the concierge's lodge. What's the building like?'

'New, modern, very smart. A tall white façade and a wrought-iron and glass front door.'

'Right. Mumble some name or other and go upstairs.'

'How will I know which apartment? . . .'

'You're right. Look, there must be a dairy somewhere near which delivers milk. Get the dairyman out of bed if you have to. Tell him a tale, preferably involving a woman.'

'Got it.'

'Can you remember how to pick a lock? Go in. Don't put any lights on. Lie low in a corner so you'd both be able to intervene if the need arises.'

'Understood, sir,' sighed poor Janvier who would probably be spending many hours keeping very still in a dark, strange apartment.

'And especially, no smoking!'

He even permitted himself a sadistic little smile. Then he chose the two men for the stake-out in Rue de Longchamp.

'Take your guns. We can't be sure how all this will turn out.'

He glanced at Colombani. The two men understood each other perfectly. This was no ordinary crook they were dealing with but the leader of a gang of killers. They had no right to take any risks.

An arrest in the bar of the Folies-Bergère, for example, would have been easier. But no one could predict how Bronsky would react. There was a good chance that he was armed and it was probable that he was the kind of man who would defend himself and even shoot into the crowd so that he could make the most of the ensuing panic.

'Who'll volunteer to go out and order beers to be brought up from the Brasserie Dauphine? And sandwiches!'

It was a sign that one of the Police Judiciaire's memorable nights was about to begin. The atmosphere of both offices in Maigret's section started to feel like that of a field HQ. Everybody was smoking, everybody was on edge. The phones were silent.

'Give me the Folies-Bergère.'

It took some time before Marchand came to the line. He had to be fetched from off the stage, where he was sorting out an argument between two exotic dancers.

'Yes, old son,' he began before he even knew who was on the line.

'Maigret.'

'Well?'

'Is he there?'

'I saw him a few moments ago.'

'Good. Don't say anything to him. Give me a ring only if he leaves by himself.'

'Will do. Don't knock him about too much will you?'

'It'll probably be someone else who'll take care of him,' replied Maigret enigmatically.

It was only a few minutes before Francine Latour would walk on to the stage of the Folies with the comic actor Dréan, at probably the same time as her lover would step into the overheated auditorium, stand for a moment at the back like a regular attender and listen with only half an ear to an exchange of dialogue which he knew by heart and to the laughter which surged from all sides.

Maria was still lying in her hospital room, tense and furious because in accordance with the rules her baby had been taken away for the night and because two policemen were standing outside, guarding the corridor. There was a further officer, just one, in another wing of the Laennec, where Pietr had just been taken after he emerged from the operating theatre.

Coméliau, in apprehensive mood, was with friends in Boulevard Saint-Germain. He had left them briefly to call Maigret.

'Still nothing?'

'A few small items. Carl Lipschitz is dead.'

'Was the shot fired by one of your men?'

'No. By one of his. The kid, Pietr, was shot in the knee by one of my inspectors.'

'So that means there's only one still on the loose?'

'Serge Madok, yes. And the leader of the bunch.'

'Whom you still haven't identified.'

'His name is Jean Bronsky.'

'Say again?'

'Bronsky.'

'Isn't he a film producer?'

'I don't know if he's actually a producer but he does dabble in cinema.'

'Just under three years ago, I had him sent down for eighteenth months.'

'That's our man.'

'Are you getting close to him?'

'At this moment he's at the Folies-Bergère.'

'Where?'

'I said: at the Folies-Bergère.'

'Aren't you going to arrest him?'

'In a while. We've got plenty of time now. I'd rather limit any damage, if you follow me.'

'Take a note of this number. I'll be here with friends until about midnight. After that I'll be at home waiting for your call.'

'I think you'll probably be able to get some sleep.'

Maigret was right. Jean Bronsky and Francine Latour first took a taxi to Maxim's for a quiet supper. It was from his office at Quai des Orfèvres that Maigret continued to follow their progress. By now it was the second time that the waiter from the Brasserie Dauphine had come up with his tray. There were dirty glasses all over the office together with half-eaten sandwiches, and the smell of tobacco smoke caught in the throat. But despite the heat, Colombani had not removed his camelhair coat, which he regarded as a kind of uniform. He also kept his hat tilted on the back of his head.

'Aren't you going to bring the woman in?'

'What woman?'

'Nine. Albert's wife.'

Maigret shook his head and looked irritated. Was this or was this not any of his business? He was quite prepared to collaborate with the people from Rue des Saussaies, provided they did not interfere.

Actually he was, for the moment, like a man feeling his way. As Monsieur Coméliau had just pointed out, he was free to arrest Jean Bronsky whenever he liked. He remembered something he had said right at the start of the inquiry, to whom he no longer remembered, with unaccustomed solemnity: 'This is a very nasty business. They are killers . . .'

Killers who all knew they had nothing to lose, so much so that if they were arrested in the middle of a crowd, and if the crowd got to know that these men were the Picardy gang, the police would not be able to prevent a lynching.

After what they had done on those farms, any jury would sentence them to death, and they knew it. Maria might, because of her child, have a slight hope of obtaining mercy from the president of the Republic.

Would she get it? It was doubtful. There was the testimony of the little girl who had survived and the evidence of the burned feet and breasts. There was the arrogance of the female, even her untamed beauty, which would weigh against her in the minds of the jury. Civilized men fear wild creatures, especially wild creatures of their own kind who remind them of life in the primeval forests of past ages. Jean Bronsky was an even more dangerous wild animal, a brutish beast dressed by the best tailor in Place Vendôme, a savage in a silk shirt who had been to university and was primed and preened every morning by a hairdresser like some peacock.

'You're playing it careful,' observed Colombani at one point, as Maigret sat patiently in front of one of the phones.

'I'm playing it careful.'

'What if he slips between our fingers?'

'I'd rather that than have one of my men gunned down.'

And thinking of which, what was the point of leaving Chevrier and his wife in their bistro out at Quai de Charenton? Phone them? They were probably in bed now. Maigret smiled and gave a shrug. Who knows? Maybe their brief masquerade was giving them a thrill, and there was no reason why they shouldn't go on playing at running a bar for another few hours.

'Hello? . . . Is that you, sir? . . . They've just gone into the Florence.'

It was the smartest club in Montmartre. Champagne *de rigueur*. Doubtless Francine Latour was wearing a new dress and had new diamonds to show off. She was very young, not yet weary of that kind of life. Are there not old women who are rich and titled and own private mansions in Avenue du Bois or in Faubourg Saint-Germain who have been going to the same nightspots for forty years?

'It's time!' said Maigret decisively.

He took his revolver out of the drawer and checked that it was loaded. Colombani looked at him and gave a faint smile.

'Want me to come along with you?'

This would be generous of Maigret. The action was

taking place in his jurisdiction. It was he who had rooted out the Picardy gang. He could have kept the job to himself and his men and thus Quai des Orfèvres would have put yet another one over on the Rue des Saussaies.

'Got your gun with you?'

'It lives in my pocket.'

Maigret's didn't. He rarely needed it.

As they crossed the courtyard, Colombani gestured towards one of the police cars.

'No. I prefer a taxi. Attracts less attention.'

He chose one carefully, one with a driver he knew, though in truth almost all the taxi-drivers knew him.

'Rue de Longchamp. Drive down it at walking speed.'

The building where Francine Latour lived stood relatively tall in the street, not far from a famous restaurant where Maigret recalled having eaten a number of good lunches. Everywhere was closed. It was now two in the morning. They needed to find a place to park. Maigret was serious, peevish and silent.

'Drive round again. Stop when I tell you to. Keep just your sidelights on, as if you're waiting to pick up a fare.'

They were less than ten metres from the apartment block. They could just make out an inspector lurking in the shadow of a carriage entrance. There had to be another officer somewhere and, up in the apartment, Janvier and his colleague were still waiting in the dark.

Maigret smoked, taking shallow pulls at his pipe. He could feel Colombani's shoulder next to his. He was sitting by the door next to the kerb.

They remained like this for forty-five minutes. Taxis

passed infrequently. At a few houses further along the street, residents returned home. Eventually a cab pulled up outside the apartment building, and a slim young man sprang on to the pavement, turned and leaned back inside to help his companion climb out.

Maigret simply said: 'Yes!'

He calculated his moves carefully. For some time his door had been slightly open, and he had kept a firm hold on the handle. With an agility no one would have expected of him, he rushed forwards and leaped on the man just as, leaning into the taxi to look at the meter, he was reaching into the pocket of his dinner-jacket for his wallet.

The young woman screamed. Maigret grabbed the man by the shoulders from behind, and his weight propelled him forwards so that they both fell on to the pavement. Maigret, who had been struck on the chin by the man's head, made a grab for Bronsky's hands to prevent him from going for his revolver. Colombani was already at his side and, cool and calm, stamped a heel into the Czech's face.

Francine Latour, still screaming for help, reached the front door of the building and started ringing the bell wildly. The two inspectors arrived at a run, and the struggle lasted for a few minutes more. Maigret was the last to get to his feet, as he had been underneath.

'Anyone injured?'

In the taxi's sidelights, blood could be seen on Maigret's hand. He looked around him then realized it had come from Bronsky's nose, which was bleeding profusely. His hands were pinned behind his back by handcuffs and this made him bend slightly forwards. There was a fierce expression on his face.

'You bastards!' he snarled.

When an inspector made as if to pay back the insult with a kick to his shins, Maigret said, as he delved into his pocket for his pipe:

'Let him get the poison off his chest. It's pretty much the only freedom he'll have from now on.'

They almost forgot Janvier and his colleague upstairs in the apartment, where, slavishly carrying out their orders, they would probably have stayed until morning.

10.

He was reporting to the commissioner of the Police Judiciaire first, which would not have exactly pleased Coméliau.

'First-rate result, Maigret. Now do me the pleasure of going home to bed. We'll take care of the details in the morning. Are we going to call in both of those stationmasters?'

From Goderville and Moucher, who would have to formally identify the man they had seen, one as he got off the train on 19 January, and the other as he got on a few hours later.

'Colombani's looking after it. They're on the way.'

Jean Bronsky was there with them, on a chair, in the office. Never had there been quite so many beers and sandwiches on the table. What surprised the Czech most was that they weren't bothering to question him.

Francine Latour was also present. She had absolutely insisted on coming because she was totally and utterly convinced that the police were making a great big mistake. So, just as an adult gives a child a book with pictures in to keep it quiet, Maigret had handed her Bronsky's file, which she was now reading, not without giving her lover horrified looks from time to time.

'What will you do now?' asked Colombani.

'Phone the examining magistrate and then I'm going home to bed.'

'Want me to drop you?'

'No thanks. Don't bother. It would only delay you.'

Maigret was up to his tricks again, and Colombani knew it. In a firm voice he gave the taxi-driver the address, Boulevard Richard-Lenoir. But a few moments later he tapped on the glass partition between the back and the front seats:

'Drive along the Seine and make for Corbeil.'

It was thus that he saw the new day break. He made out the first anglers as they took up their positions on the banks of the river, from which a faint mist rose. He saw the first barges blocking the approaches to the locks and the smoke that was beginning to drift up from the houses into a mother-of-pearl sky.

'You'll come to an inn somewhere a little way upstream,' he said after they had passed Corbeil.

They found it. Its well-shaded terrace looked out on to the Seine, and the inn itself was surrounded by leafy alcoves where people came in droves on Sundays. The proprietor, a man with a long red moustache, was emptying a boat and fishing nets were spread over the floating landing-stage.

After the kind of night he had just had, it was a pleasure to walk through the dewy grass and breathe in the scent of the earth, the smell of logs burning in a hearth and see the maid, her hair not yet done, toing and froing in the kitchen.

'Is there any coffee?'

'In a few minutes, though really we aren't open.'

'Does your paying guest usually come down early?'

'I've been hearing her moving around her room for some time. Listen.'

And indeed they both could hear the sound of footsteps coming from above the ceiling with its stout, exposed beams.

'It's her coffee that I'm just making.'

'Lay the table for two.'

'Are you a friend of hers?'

'I should say so. I'd be surprised if I wasn't.'

And a friend he proved to be. It happened very simply. When he introduced himself and gave his rank, she was briefly frightened. But he spoke in a kindly voice:

'Would you mind if I had my breakfast with you?'

Two places were set on a table by the window: solid earthenware plates on a red-chequered cloth. The coffee steamed in bowls. The butter had a taste of hazelnuts to it.

She had a cast in her eye, of course, a heavy, terrible cast, and she knew it. When he looked straight at her, she was discomforted, felt ashamed and explained:

'When I was seventeen, my mother made me have an operation because my left eye was turning inwards. After the operation, it looked outwards. The surgeon suggested redoing it, free of charge. But I said no.'

Oddly enough, after a couple of minutes, it was hardly noticeable. It was even possible to think she was almost pretty.

'Poor Albert! If you'd only known him! Such a cheerful, kindly man, always eager to please other people.'

'He was your cousin, wasn't he?'

'A very distant cousin.'

Her accent too had a charm of its own. The overriding impression she gave was that she felt an immense need for kindness. It was not an appeal for kindness to be shown her, but a need to spread kindness all around her.

'I was nearly thirty. Both my parents were dead. I was on the shelf. They didn't leave me much, and I had never worked. I came to Paris because I was unhappy living all by myself in our big house. I hardly knew Albert. I had only heard about him. I went to see him.'

Of course she did. And he understood. Albert was alone too. She had probably made a great fuss of him, and he wasn't used to it.

'If you knew how much I loved him! Of course I never expected that he would love me too. I knew that could never be. But he made me believe that he did. And I pretended I did believe him, just to please him. We were happy, inspector. I'm sure he was happy. He had no reason not to be, did he? And we'd just celebrated our wedding anniversary. I don't know what happened that day at the races. He left me in the stand every time he went off to place a bet. Once when he came back he seemed to have something on his mind and from then on he began looking all around him, as if he was watching out for somebody. He insisted that we came home in a taxi and he kept turning round. When we got to our place, he told the driver: "Keep going!", though why, I don't know. So on we went as far as Place de la Bastille. There he got out. He said: "Go home by yourself. I'll be there in an hour or two." It was because he was being followed. He didn't come home that night. He phoned to say he'd be back the next morning. The following day he phoned twice . . .'

'That was Wednesday?'

'That's right. The second time it was to say I wasn't to stay in and wait for him but to go to the cinema. I didn't want to, but he insisted. He almost got angry with me. So I went. Have you arrested them?'

'All except one, and it won't be long before we get him. He's on his own now, and I don't think he's dangerous, especially since we know who he is and what he looks like.'

Maigret was unaware of how true his words were. At that very moment, a member of the Vice Squad was arresting Serge Madok in a licensed brothel on Boulevard de La Chapelle – actually, an unspeakably filthy hole frequented mainly by Arabs – where he had been holed up since the previous evening and had stubbornly refused to leave.

He offered no resistance. He was more or less dead to the world, being helplessly drunk. He had to be carried out to the police van.

'What will you do now?' Maigret asked gently as he filled his pipe.

'I don't know. I expect I'll go back home, to where I came from. I can't run a restaurant on my own. Now I have nobody.'

She repeated that last word and looked around her as if she were looking for someone to be kind to.

'I don't know what I'm going to do with my life.'

'Ever thought of adopting?'

She looked up, at first in disbelief and then she smiled.

'Do you think I might . . . that they'd let me have a . . . that . . . ?'

The idea was taking root in her mind and in her heart so quickly that Maigret was frightened. It was not exactly that he had spoken without thinking, rather all he had really wanted to do was discover how the land lay. It was just a thought he had had on the way in the taxi, one of those fanciful, bold thoughts which seem like good ideas when we are half asleep or utterly exhausted, but in the cold light of day look quite mad.

'We'll discuss it some other time. Because I shall see you again, if you wish . . . In any case, I have some financial matters to settle with you, because we took the liberty of opening your restaurant . . .'

'Do you know of a child who . . .'

'Well now, there is one, actually, who in a few weeks or months from now might well have no mother.'

She flushed bright red, but he was left red-faced too: he was kicking himself for being so stupid as to raise the issue.

'A baby, is it?' she stammered.

'Yes, a very small one.'

'He'll be helpless, then.'

'Quite helpless.'

'And he won't necessarily be like . . .'

'You must excuse me, now. It's time I was getting back to Paris.'

'I'll think about it.'

'Don't think about it too much. I'm cross with myself

for having spoken to you about it.'

'No, you did right. Could I see him? Tell me, would they let me?'

'May I ask you one more question? Albert told me over the phone that you knew me. I don't remember ever having seen you before.'

'But I saw you once, a long time ago, when I was just twenty. My mother was still alive and we were on holiday in Dieppe.'

'The Hôtel Beauséjour!' he exclaimed.

He had stayed there for a fortnight with Madame Maigret.

'All the people staying at the hotel talked about you and stared when you weren't looking . . .'

He felt quite odd in the taxi, which was now taking him back to Paris through country flooded with bright sunshine. New buds were beginning to appear in the hedges.

'It might be rather pleasant to get away for a holiday,' he thought, perhaps because of the memories of Dieppe which Nine had just revived.

He knew that he would do nothing of the sort, for this was something which happened to him from time to time. It was like a cold which he could cure by treating it with large amounts of work.

The suburbs . . . The bridge at Joinville . . .

'Go along Quai de Charenton.'

The bar was open. Chevrier looked rather embarrassed.

'I'm glad you came, sir. They phoned to say it's all over. My wife is wondering if she has to go and do her shopping.'

'As she pleases.'

'But there's no point now?'

'None at all.'

'They also asked me if I'd seen you. It seems they've been phoning you at home and everywhere else. Do you want to call HQ?'

Maigret paused. This time he really was exhausted and wanted only one thing: his own bed and the sensual pleasure of sliding into a bottomless, dreamless sleep.

'I bet I shall sleep for a solid twenty-four hours.'

But, alas, it would not happen! Someone would disturb him before he managed it. They had got into too much of a habit at Quai des Orfèvres – and he had let it happen – of saying at the first sign of trouble: 'Ring Maigret!'

'Can I get you anything, sir?'

'A calvados, since you insist.'

All this had started with calvados. Might as well finish it on the same note.

'Hello? Who's that?'

It was Bodin. Maigret had forgotten Bodin. He had probably also forgotten a number of others who would still be standing guard pointlessly at different locations across Paris.

'I've got the letter.'

'What letter?'

'The one from the poste restante.'

'Oh yes! Good.'

Poor Bodin. His great discovery wasn't making much of an impact.

'Would you like me to open it and tell you what's in the envelope?'

'If you like.'

'Wait a minute . . . There . . . No written message, just a railway ticket.'

'Right.'

'You knew?'

'I had my suspicions. It's a first-class return from Goderville to Paris.'

'Correct. We've got some stationmasters waiting for you here.'

'That's Colombani's department.'

Maigret sipped his calvados and smiled a faint smile. Another side of the character of Li'l Albert, whom he had not known when he was alive but had in a sense rebuilt piece by piece.

Like a certain breed of race-goers, Albert couldn't help keeping his eyes down, on the ground, which was littered with losing Mutuel betting slips. Among them a man may sometimes find a winning slip which has been thrown away by mistake.

It wasn't a winning slip he had found that morning but a train ticket.

If such had not been his habit . . . If he hadn't seen the man from whose pocket it had dropped . . . If the name Goderville had not instantly made him think of the massacres perpetrated by the Picardy gang . . . If his feelings had not been written on his face . . .

'Poor Albert!' sighed Maigret.

. . . he would still be alive. On the other hand, a few more old farmers and their wives would have passed from life into death, but not before they had had the soles of their feet scorched by Maria.

'My wife says she'd rather shut up shop straight away,' said Chevrier.

'Close up then.'

After that there were streets, a meter which showed an astronomical figure, Madame Maigret, who seemed to him a trifle less sweet-tempered after that brief time spent with Nine and, as he snuggled down between the sheets, put her foot firmly down:

'This time, I'm taking the phone off the hook and I'm not opening the door to anyone.'

He heard the beginning of the sentence but never found out how it ended.

Other Titles in the Series

THE TWO-PENNY BAR
GEORGES SIMENON

A radiant late afternoon. The sunshine almost as thick as syrup in the quiet streets of the Left Bank . . . there are days like this, when ordinary life seems heightened, when the people walking down the street, the trams and cars all seem to exist in a fairy tale.

A story told by a condemned man leads Maigret to a bar by the Seine and into the sleazy underside of respectable Parisian life. In the oppressive heat of summer, a forgotten crime comes to life.

Translated by David Watson

Previously published as *The Bar on the Seine*

OTHER TITLES IN THE SERIES

THE SHADOW PUPPET
GEORGES SIMENON

'One by one the lighted windows went dark. The silhouette of the dead man could still be seen through the frosted glass like a Chinese shadow puppet . . . A young woman crossed the courtyard with hurried steps, leaving a whiff of perfume in her wake.'

Summoned to the dimly-lit Place des Vosges one night, Maigret uncovers a tragic story of desperate lives, unhappy families, addiction and a terrible, fatal greed.

Translated by Ros Schwartz

INSPECTOR MAIGRET

OTHER TITLES IN THE SERIES

LOCK N° 1
GEORGES SIMENON

'*There was amusement in Ducrau's eyes. In the inspector's too. They stood looking at each other with the same stifled mirth which was full of unspoken thoughts, perhaps of defiance and maybe too of an odd respect.*'

A man hauled out of the Charenton canal one night; a girl wandering, confused, in a white nightdress … these events draw Maigret into the world of the charismatic self-made businessman Ducrau, and the misdeeds of his past.

Translated by David Coward

www.penguin.com

OTHER TITLES IN THE SERIES

MAIGRET
GEORGES SIMENON

'It was indeed Maigret who was beside him, smoking his pipe, his velvet collar upturned, his hat perched on his head. But it wasn't an enthusiastic Maigret. It wasn't even a Maigret who was sure of himself.'

Maigret's peaceful retirement in the country is interrupted when his nephew comes to him for help after being implicated in a crime he didn't commit. Soon Maigret is back in the heart of Paris, and out of place in a once-familiar world...

Translated by Ros Schwartz

Other Titles in the Series

CÉCILE IS DEAD
GEORGES SIMENON

'Barely twenty-eight years old. But it would be difficult to look more like an old maid, to move less gracefully, no matter how hard she tried to be pleasing. Those black dresses . . . that ridiculous green hat!'

For six months the dowdy Cécile has been coming to the police station, desperate to convince them that someone has been breaking into her aunt's apartment. No one takes her seriously – until Maigret unearths a story of merciless, deep-rooted greed.

Translated by Anthea Bell

OTHER TITLES IN THE SERIES

Pietr the Latvian
The Late Monsieur Gallet
The Hanged Man of Saint-Pholien
The Carter of *La Providence*
The Yellow Dog
Night at the Crossroads
A Crime in Holland
The Grand Banks Café
A Man's Head
The Dancer at the Gai-Moulin
The Two-Penny Bar
The Shadow Puppet
The Saint-Fiacre Affair
The Flemish House
The Madman of Bergerac
The Misty Harbour
Liberty Bar
Lock No. 1
Maigret
Cécile is Dead
The Cellars of the Majestic
The Judge's House
Signed, Picpus
Inspector Cadaver

And more to follow

www.penguin.com